A black and white movie is a film of contrasts – of shadows and lightness – of good and evil.

Sublime upon sublime
scarcely presents a
contrast, and we need a
little rest from everything,
even the beautiful.
~ Victor Hugo ~

Other books by this author:

Written as Ellen Joy Rickerd:
<u>America's Family Tree</u>

Written as Gere G. Johnson
<u>The Guardian Spirit</u>

LIFE IS A
BLACK & WHITE MOVIE

Gere G. Johnson

Published through CreateSpace at Amazon.com

Black & White Movie

IBSN: 1449501087
EAN: 9781449501082

This book is dedicated to great dads everywhere but especially to my own, Mel Johnson.

And to my son, Scott, and my brothers Norman and Jim, and to my nephew, Michael, and to my husband, Rod.

Acknowledgements, Credits, & Thanks to:

Kristen Asmus, Managing Editor <u>GSA Today</u>: thanks for your help with Spanish words and phrases and for all the endless proof-reading

Scott Azmus, Astronomy & Geology teacher and owner of "Applegarth Books" in Millington, Tennessee, for all things about telescopes and astronomy

Connie Joy Evans for entering and winning my "Be a Character" contest.

John W. Hanlin, Sheriff Douglas County, Oregon, for information about legal charges and jail terms

Tim Kosderka, Forest Manager, Roseburg District, Weyerhaeuser Company, for information about Oregon State Forestry management rules

Robert Mah, Berkeley, California: thanks for your help with all things Chinese, especially Chinese cooking, and for being a model.

- ✓ Many pictures on cover and on the text pages from: www.dreamstime.com and from author's collection;
- ✓ Pictures on page 144 from: Kristen Asmus;
- ✓ Fire photos flickr.com/photos/smokeshowing;
- ✓ Cover design by the author.

As always, I thank everyone who helped with the writing of this book. All omissions, errors, and just plain doltishness is entirely my own.

1. Andrew/André

Andrew Higgins Miller was born in January 1933 and lived most of his childhood in Concord, California, where his father worked at the Naval Weapons Station at Port Chicago (NAVWPNSTA), and his mother was a waitress at the Treasure House – a greasy-spoon eatery frequented by the locals as well as the Navy personnel. They served the best hamburgers in town and had great homemade pie as well.

Andrew's mother and father never married, and when Seaman Second Class Miller was transferred to another station, Andrew and his mother, Eileen, stayed in Concord. It was a nice enough town – it had not yet grown into the bedroom community that it is now, for no one in the 1930's or 1940's would have been crazy enough to commute all the way to work in Oakland or San Francisco (a trip of twenty-three or thirty-six miles respectively – too far to drive just to work).

Eileen Higgins went to the Navy people when Andrew's father left and demanded (and got) a monthly allotment check for the half-Navy child she was raising. This, along with her earnings from the waitress job, kept the two of them quite nicely. She also had no problem replacing Andrew's father in her love life. All the Navy guys said she was a "looker" with her long blond hair and blue eyes. They said she looked like Betty Grable, and she was not shy about showing off her own well-shaped legs. In addition, Andrew was a cute kid with light blond hair and the intensely blue eyes that he inherited from his mother. Eileen taught him at an early age that if he looked happy and acted charming, he would get a lot more attention – and a lot more quarters from the guys in her life.

After the war, when Andrew was twelve, Eileen finally met a man who wanted to marry her and be a father to Andrew. Mr. Howard Jackson was a good man. He'd been in the war as a diesel mechanic on a submarine and now had a good job in Oakland working as a shop smith at a paper company. He had to keep all of their machinery up and working so that they could produce their particularly fine quality drafting paper. The postwar nation was in a growing mode and many architects and draftsmen needed that paper.

Howard bought a house for them in nearby Berkeley when Eileen got pregnant and it became obvious that they needed a bigger place than the little apartment they had been living in. Andrew thought the house on Milvia Street was really copasetic, as Mom would say. He loved running up and down the stairs or sliding down the banister. Downstairs was a parlor with a small fireplace and a dining room along with a kitchen and utility room. He had a nice room with a closet of his very own on the second floor next to the bathroom, and he could look out his window and see everything the neighbors were doing in their kitchen and sometimes in their bedroom if they didn't remember to close the curtains. There was a good backyard for playing catch with Mr. Jackson, who got a couple of mitts and a ball. Andy was a natural athlete and could really zip that ball into Mr. Jackson's mitt. Whap! The best part of it was that the house was within walking distance to school and to Telegraph Avenue (which was where the "action" was).

This was when Andrew met his friend, Robert Fung-Liú. Robert knew everything there was to know about getting along in Berkeley and in San Francisco, and he taught Andy (as he was now

called) how to get away with not going to school regularly and how to meet girls … especially "easy" girls. Andy had grown to six feet two inches of tanned, blond, blue-eyed devil, and the girls loved him! Robert also taught him about how to get people to pay him for tours of The City. There was a Chinese man over there who had been in several movies during the war, and he advertised the

tours – except that he had the boys do the work while he raked in the money. However, it was a great way to make a few bucks, and Andy really wasn't competition for Robert, who took groups on tours of Chinatown.

Andy wouldn't have been so welcome there – so he took people on tours, by way of the cable car system, of Fisherman's Wharf, Union Square, Coit Tower, Golden Gate Park, the Palace of Fine Arts, and places like that. The two teenagers took the bus across the bay to The City whenever Andy could skip school or sneak out in the evening or on the weekends. The most lucrative times were when they got to The City in the evening and met the folks just getting off the Gray Line tours – people who were from the country and too afraid to poke around town by themselves. Some of the men traveling alone would even ask the boys to point them towards after-tour "private action." The two teenagers made enough money to keep them in cigarettes and to take girls out to dinner and movies.

Eileen and Howard worried about Andy and what he might be up to, but they were very busy by now with their adorable little twin girls, Ashley and Olivia. The twins were the focus of their lives, and Andy was generally free to keep whatever hours he liked and come and go as he pleased. However, by the grace of God or maybe just because he was a really bright and talented kid, Andrew did manage to graduate from Berkeley High School in 1951. He had a steady girlfriend, Betsy, but he soon forgot about her when he was drafted by the Army and left for training and then to the war in Korea.

Andy spent two **long** years in Korea … slogging up one hill after another … only to be pushed back down again by the Chinese Communists. Peace talks went on for all of the two years that Andy was being shot at. The Korean War was the first armed confrontation of the Cold War and set the standard for many later conflicts. It created the idea of a proxy war, where the two super-powers would fight in another country, forcing the people in that nation to suffer the bulk of the destruction and death involved in a war between such large nations. It was called the "coldest" war not just because of the the frigid winters but also because of the indiscriminate killing of civilians by both sides of the conflict.

Andy came home from the war greatly changed, and he came home with a Purple Heart because of the huge scar on his belly caused when a female North Korean infiltrator-whore had tried to eviscerate him with his own bayonet while he was asleep. Of course, that's not the story he told. His version was much more colorful – about charging at a group of Koreans who had run out of ammo and how they had tried to kill him with a knife before he could "shoot every damned one of them."

Andy found his old friend, Robert, and the two of them started on a life of moving from place to place and from identity to identity. They went to San Francisco, Las Vegas, and Los Angeles, trying to figure out how to make a bunch of money and where they could meet rich women. Both answered the question in unison: "Beverly Hills."

They opened their first storefront on Rodeo Drive, and paid half down on the rent, telling the owner they'd have the rest in ten days. The partners invested in some equipment and some decorative plants and put an "Open" sign in the window – for the "Oriental Youth and Fitness Salon." The Salon offered exercise routines, massages, facials, Oriental herbal cures as well as advice on Feng Shui, the flow of the chi, and even I Ching readings.

The business was immediately successful. Women who were no longer as young and shapely as Hollywood starlets flocked to Mr. Andrew and Mr.

Robert for treatments and were willing to pay whatever was asked in order to stay young and preserve their marriages. Too many husbands strayed anyway, but there were always young men willing to "escort" the older women, and Andy and Robert could supply them whenever asked.

The salon was so successful, in fact, that the partners decided to open branch offices in Las Vegas and San Francisco. They then offered their clients franchise operations. Licensees paid between $30,000 and $68,000 and were assured income of between $500 and $200 per week. The two men deposited over $1 million in a bank in San Francisco's Chinatown in one year. The licensees never made the profit that was promised because they didn't have Mr. Andrew and Mr. Robert and didn't know about the escort business portion of the salon. But no legal action was ever filed because of the vague language of the contract, which actually promised nothing.

During this period, André Zhalovy was "born," though he developed over a long period of time. Andy was a natural and easy liar. In fact, he was incurably dishonest. He found that making up stories about himself, his background, and his family made him more interesting to people. Gradually, he became André, a Russian Jew who had spent a lot of time in Israel, who was a former KGB agent, who had escaped from a Chinese prison camp, and who now poured out his angst and torment in books about being a spy for the Soviet Union in Israel, Korea, and China. André was a very clever writer and was able to produce thrilling, riveting page-turners. He wrote quickly and soon became very successful and famous He also took up a brush and painted – in the post impressionist manner. He thought his work was a lot like Cezanne. He painted nudes, almost entirely, but occasionally he'd do a still life just to show that he could; however, his books sold better and faster than his art.

2. Vivienne

In 1999, at the height of his fame as a writer and artist, André met Vivienne Audier Ridgeway, a rich widow and San Francisco socialite who wanted to move to her "ranch" in Oregon. He saw her as slightly too old for him (she was seventy to his sixty-six), but he could see dollar bills written all over her. And for the first time in his life he got married. He'd never gone long without a woman. His fame and good looks had always been like catnip to the girls.

He vaguely remembered some of them: the beautiful Miss Chinatown, Daisy Dxiang Lee, who had the most lovely doll-like quality. He'd met her through Robert, of course. Then there was Mary Margaret Griffith, the gorgeous little Catholic girl in her paraochial school uniform, and, of course, Dorothy Lerner, a wealthy married woman in Marin County. Naturally, there were others – many others, but he couldn't possibly remember them all. These were just the ones he'd spent more than one night with. He'd left some of them when he thought they might be pregnant, but he wasn't sure. How could he conceivably be sure?

At any rate, the newly married couple moved to Vivienne's house to settle down. Vivienne called her house "Daffodil Hill" because she had planted hundreds of bulbs on the grassy hill where the house stood, a knoll in the middle of her prime acreage near the Umpqua River in southwestern Oregon. Her husband had been a doctor and a real estate speculator. He'd told Vivienne that he'd bought the land "for a song" from a poor sap who had no idea of its worth, and they had built a small house on it.

Vivienne was tall and quite thin. She was a perfect "hanger" for French couture. She hated the San Francisco dinner parties where she had to carry on a conversation with other doctor's wives and even pretend to like the food that was served. She much preferred cocktail parties where all she had to do was drink and make small talk – nonsense talk. People thought she was delightfully French, and having that heritage, she could drink all evening without having it affect her.

Vivienne had had a couple of face lifts, but her baggy, saggy neck was a dead giveaway to her aging. So she had several beautiful choker/collars made – some out of pearls or emeralds or semi-precious stones and all with platinum – never gold. Her hair was pure white (which she high-lighted with a little lavender rinse), so gold just didn't look right. Her everyday collars (all meant to fit around her neck and hide the sagging) were made usually of fabric or beads. She never went out in public without make up or without one of her collars.

André was no longer involved with Robert in any business venture. Robert was successful and retired now in Palm Springs or Palm Desert or some "damned Palm thing." And André, of course, was also retired, though he did still paint. Vivienne was perfectly willing to pose for him, and he did do one portrait of her which they hung over one of the fireplaces. It wasn't like his usual stuff. He did this one with sharp lines and pastel colors. Vivienne quite liked it, but since André preferred to do nudes, Vivienne didn't mind when he hired models to sit for him.

The house no longer seemed large enough for everything that the two busy people wanted to do. They added to the house several times …until they had a large whimsically outlandish house. One of the bizarre features was the access to the second floor – which could only be accomplished by going outside and up the stairs – they hadn't wanted to ruin the "feng shui" of the downstairs by putting stairs there. There was a flight of stairs on each side of the house, and they were

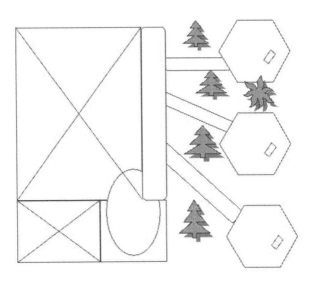

protected (somewhat) from the weather by the roof's three foot overhang. The downstairs was really just one room with two huge fireplaces – one at each end of the room. The kitchen was open to the main area, and the living spaces were only evident because of the furniture placement.　　There was also an indoor-outdoor swimming pool – just a quick dive though a short tunnel brought one from the small indoor pool to the larger outdoor one.

At one time there had only been a studio for André on the northeast side of the house plus three bedrooms and four bathrooms – all upstairs – but Andy and Vivienne added three small pentagonal cottages (each with its own bathroom) that connected to the main house through plexiglass and steel covered walkways. The huge old Douglas firs stood around the house and between the cottages. It was a place to live, refresh, and rethink life.

Vivenne was a Jewish French woman who had spent the World War II years hidden in a Catholic convent along with her little sister, Marie. The rest of her family had not been hidden and had not survived the Nazis. After the war, Vivienne and Marie had been sent to the United States to live with their American relatives, the Franz Audier family, in California. Vivienne was old enough by then to have a job as a French teacher, and her family arranged for her to have the proper papers to show her education at the nunnery.

She went right to work at an all-girl college in Northern California, Mills College. She was an excellent teacher, and everyone liked her. She soon had her little sister move in with her in a nice apartment in the Oakland Hills. Marie finished high school and enrolled at Mills College to take a degree in history. No one knew they were Jewish, and they didn't tell anyone. It just didn't seem the prudent thing to do.

Marie met a University of California student who was studying engineering on the GI bill, and they soon married. After he received his master's degree, she and her new husband moved to Livermore, which was out in the valley and where there was some sort of government facility that employed a lot of engineers.

It wasn't really much after that when Vivienne met her own husband. He had studied biology at Berkeley and then took a medical degree at the University in San Francisco. They married while he was struggling through his surgical residency. His little sister was one of Vivienne's students, and she made sure that her big brother met her favorite teacher. Dr. and Mrs. Ridgeway became prominent members of Bay Area society as he opened his practice in San Francisco, and she gave up teaching to become a chic French fashion-plate wife. They frequented the opera and the ballet. She was always dressed like a lovely French model with the splendid and showy jewelry and furs that the doctor encouraged her to wear.

In the course of his career, Dr. Ridgeway made a lot of money and invested a great deal of it in real estate. He bought office buildings. He bought tracts where middle-class housing could be constructed. He bought land in Oregon where he had a house built on a hill in the middle of the forest, and he bought a "cottage" in Hawaii where they could vacation whenever they wanted to. They lived well. They lived happily. They drank a lot. They smoked a lot. He ate a lot. And Dr. Ridgeway died on the golf course in Beverly Hills when he was sixty-nine years old.

Since they'd never had any children, Vivienne now found herself alone. She certainly had no money problems, but she hadn't aged well, and was no longer the beautiful French woman she had been. She had to hire escorts to go with her to the various functions that she'd become accustomed to attending. That caused a stir with the other women, and it wasn't really very comfortable for Vivienne either. That was when she met the enormously charming writer, André Zhalovy. He was fascinating to be with. He'd been just everywhere and knew everyone who counted. And he was Jewish – what a relief it would be to be able to be openly Jewish again instead of pretending to be Goy.

At this point in his life, André was no longer the highly successful writer he had once been. He often drank too much and couldn't concentrate, but when he was sober, he was still the con-man/shark he'd always been. He talked Vivienne into unloading all the real estate that the doctor had invested in. He told her that that the market was too high in California and would break "one of these days" and then she'd be out everything. So she put all the money into their various joint accounts, and they concentrated just on the property in Oregon and on fixing that house the way they wanted it.

In 2005 Vivienne was diagnosed with ovarian cancer. It was a terrible time for them because they both knew that the survival rate from that particular cancer was very, very low. The only silver lining was that it quickly got both of them to stop smoking. André hired a nurse to take care of his wife and watched as she took the radiation and chemotherapy with the illness quickly eating her up in spite of them. She had no fat on her body and she had no strength with which to fight the disease. She died a painful death in 2006.

André inherited everything. Her only living relative, Marie, did not contest that. She was comfortable in her own right and knew what a faithful companion André had been, especially during the dreadful illness and death of her sister. André fired Vivienne's nurse and housekeeper. He took down her portrait and stored it in the garage along with a lot of his other paintings. He was alone and rich and didn't want any reminders of how he got that way.

He sat in the house and drank by the hour. He didn't eat unless one of Vivienne's friends brought something over. He was slovenly. He didn't bathe because no one reminded him to do so. His drunkeness and loneliness finally broke him down into a crying, slobbering mess lying alone on the floor of a filthy, cluttered house. When he roused from his oblivian, he could not tolerate the smell of himself or the smell of the house.

Vivienne had turned his darkness to light, but he didn't realize it until she was long gone.

He dragged himself up off the floor and up the stairs to the unused second floor bathroom – and wondered to himself where he had relieved himself during the previous period of stupor. He soaped and showered and stood under the purifiying torrent until the water turned cold. He toweled off, put on clean clothes, and threw away the old ones. As soon as he got back downstairs, he opened all the windows and started throwing trash into giant black bags to go to the dump – bottles – lots of bottles, plus pizza boxes and Chinese food boxes with green mossy growth inside. Much of the trash he couldn't even identify, but he threw it in the bags and then threw the bags outside.

Then he finally noticed that he was hungry …very hungry. He opened the refrigerator and found beer – a bounty of beer and catsup, mustard, pickles, moldy strawberry jam (which he threw out), and nothing else. The freezer was not much better – coffee beans, ice cubes, and a bottle of vodka.

No. He was not going to make a meal out of vodka, beer, and pickles. He found the keys to his Cadillac Escalade and, after a little work, got it started and backed up to the front door of the house. He threw all the black bags in the back, locked the house door, and drove off towards the dump and thence to town.

He sat down in the first eatery that he ran into on his drive into town (after the dump) and ordered a big cheeseburger, french fries, a chocolate shake, and a piece of coconut cream pie plus a cup of coffee. He sat there and ate lustily without even looking up until he got to the pie and coffee. When he did look up, he offered the waitress a job cleaning his house and being his companion. She was an older woman – maybe fifty and plump – she would be safe from him. Not his type.

She told him, "No thanks, Mr. Zhalovy. Yeah, I know who you are, and I wouldn't spend a night in your house with you – even if I was desperate."

"Gee, thanks," André said, "Well, do you know anyone who might be interested in a job?"

"Yup, as a matter of fact I do. My niece, Cloud. She's a little strange – has everything that can be pierced with some sort of stud in it – but she's a hard worker and brighter than she might seem at first," the waitress answered.

"Send her out to the house. You know where it is. And I'll talk to her." And that's how Cloud got to be a member of the household.

At first she was grossed-out by how dirty and smelly the house was, but as promised by her aunt, she went right to work scrubbing, scouring, washing, and dusting. She also looked into the cupboards, the refrigerator, and the freezer, borrowed the SUV and went to the supermarket. She bought $200 worth of food and supplies and then made a salad and grilled a steak for André's dinner and one for herself as well.

3. Cloud

Even with Cloud living in the same house,
 André was lonely. He and Cloud talked a lot – about philosophy, about religion, about politics and even her love life. She was a very bright girl, but she was largely uneducated. She had her GED (general equivalency diploma), but she had little knowledge of history or of current events and had never actually read a whole book. In fact, she didn't believe there were any books in her home. This was a tragic situation, André thought, and he showed her to his collection of books – recommending the ones he thought she should start with. He made her a reading list and told her to feel free to use the dictionary when she didn't understand a word. If that didn't help, she should come to him or call the library. He told her that the librarians were paid to look up stuff for people. In any case, he said they would discuss her reading each night at dinner since this reading was now part of her job description and the hours spent on it would be paid

just like the hours spent cleaning, cooking, shopping, and everything else.

ANDRÉ S READING LIST FOR CLOUD:

How the Garcia Girls Lost their Accents, by Julia Alvarez
I Know Why the Caged Bird Sings, by Maya Angelou
Jane Eyre, by Charlotte Bronte
The Great Gatsby, by F. Scott Fitzgerald
The Sun Also Rises, by Ernest Hemingway
A Separate Peace, by John Knowles
To Kill A Mockingbird, by Harper Lee
Beloved, by Toni Morrison
Animal Farm, by George Orwell
Frankenstein, by Mary Shelley
The Joy Luck Club, by Amy Tan
The Hobbit, by J.R.R. Tolkien
Anna Karenina, by Leo Tolstoy
Slaugherhouse-Five, by Kurt Vonnegut
I, Robot, by Isaac Asimov
Illustrated Man, by Ray Bradbury
Crystal Cave, by Mary Stewart
QB VII, by Leon Uris

That should keep her busy, he thought, and it would make for very good dinnertime conversation. Thinking about it, André realized that it had been so long since he'd read some of those books, he might have to refresh his memory in order to have intelligent comments to make. For some reason, Cloud selected Beloved by Toni Morrison to read first. When they talked about that, she said she picked it because the title was beautiful, but the inside wasn't anything like what she expected. So far she'd only read a little, but it was "real sad."

André was still drinking and still making a mess of the house every night. Cloud drove up to the house every morning in her beat up old 1987 Plymouth Horizon. She arrived in time to make him a breakfast each day, and required him to sit down and eat it. She usually made eggs, bacon, toast, and orange juice. Then she cleaned up after him when he vomited every morning. She kept telling him that he was going to have to change his ways.

Often Cloud said, "You are a stinking, worthless son-of-a-bitch. No one wants to be around you unless you pay them to do it – and you don't hardly pay me enough to put up with you day after day."

Sometimes when he was still just mellow but not yet pain-free, André would think about his life. Where and how had he screwed it up so badly? How did he end up being a stinking drunk? He thought about the great times with Robert and the money they made with that "Youth Salon" business. Those were the good old days, he thought. "I was young then – and virile – and had as many women as I wanted. Sometimes I took one out to breakfast, one to lunch, and one to dinner – and 'had' each one afterwards. Whew!"

But then Robert went his own way, and good old Andrew Miller ceased to be and was replaced by André Zhalovy. Of course, there were still plenty of good times as he became a famous author. The fame was definite **chick-bait**. Vivienne ruined all that. Yes, it was Vivienne's fault. Sure he'd dallied a little after they married, but it wasn't the same. He was tied down. He was a prime bull with a ring in his nose and a chain fastened to Vivienne's little finger – her stupid, well-manicured little finger!

But wait a minute, he thought, Vivienne was the one with the money, wasn't she? Who were the others?

Did any of the others have any money? Probably not, he thought, because if they did, he might have married one or more of them. He wished he knew where they were. He wished he knew where Robert was. If he had Robert here or if he had any family here at all, he might not drink as much. Might not.

He thought about this more and more every day, and he drank a little less each day until finally the day came when he ate his entire breakfast and didn't throw up. Cloud was very pleased with him. He was still a little shaky, but he thought he might be able to hold a paint brush again.

He asked her, "Would you pose for me, Cloud? I might try painting again if you'd pose for me."

She said, "Guess I could – but you'd have to pay me extra. I've seen some of your paintings, and those women sure don't wear much."

"Oh, I don't know. Maybe I'll try something different this time." And he did paint her once. She had her clothes on, but he painted her nude as he imagined she would look.[i]

He kept thinking about Robert and about family. He became obsessed with the idea of having family around. He wondered whether he had any children. He had no idea.

He asked Cloud, "How would I go about finding out whether I have any family?"

She suggested, "Just Google them and see if they're still around. Want me to do that for you?"

"Uhmm, no. To tell you the truth, none of them would have the same name as I have. I changed my name years ago when I started writing. I don't know how I would go about finding anyone. My original name was Miller, and that's got to be a really common name, right?"

"Probably," she said, "but you try it. There's so much information on the Internet these days, you know. Just go to Google.com and type in the name you're looking for – like maybe your own old name. It might lead you to someone."

"You think so?"

"Well, it can't hurt to try. And if all else fails you could hire a private eye – like on TV – give him the facts and nothing but the facts, and see what he turn up for you."

4. Family

The bond
that links your true family
is not one of blood, but
of respect and joy in
each other's life.
Rarely do members
of one family grow up
under the same
roof.[ii]

And so André did it. After trying briefly and unsuccessfully to find some family and friends on the internet, he hired an almost-ethical detective (is that an oxymoron?) he had known during his early days as André Zhalovy. He told the man what he could remember of the people that stood out in his mind:

1. Robert Fung-Liú, his Chinese friend from Berkeley. He thought he ended up in Palm Springs or Palm Desert – not sure.
2. Daisy Dxiang Lee, who had been Miss Chinatown San Francisco in 1956. Her family had been quite influential in the Chinese community of the city.
3. Mary Margaret Griffith, who was a lovely Catholic high school girl in 1965. He knew nothing about her family except that they had lived at the time in Santa Barbara.
4. Dorothy Ruth Lerner, who was married to a wealthy lawyer and lived in Marin County – probably Tiburon – in 1973 when he knew her.

It took a long time; nevertheless, with just those few clues, the detective was able to track down three children: Joy Lee Aiello of San Francisco, Mary Kathryn Miller of Northridge, California, and Maxwell Jacob Lerner (deceased). But the young Maxwell did have a wife, Deirdre (Dolly) Taylor Lerner and a grandson, Luke, now living in Yreka, California. He was still tracking Robert. He had apparently moved around a lot.

André was very happy that he now felt like he had a family – at least he had names, addresses, and phone numbers. But he was reluctant to personally contact them – perhaps scare them. So he called his attorney and asked him to handle the family for him.

The firm of Weber, Stevens & Evans immediately fired off very simply stated introductory letters to each of the women:

Weber, Stevens & Evans P.C.
235 NE Hoyt
Portland, OR 97213
503-555-7634
www.weberstevensevans.com

April 3, 2008

Mrs. Joy Aiello, San Francisco, California
Mrs. Deirdre Lerner, Yreka, California
Miss Mary Kathryn Miller, Northridge, California

To each above named person:

I am the attorney of record for Mr. André Zhalovy of Oregon. Mr. Zhalovy asserts the following:

1. That he was formerly known as Andrew Higgins Miller.

2. That he is the biological father of Joy Aiello, Mary Kathryn Miller, and the deceased Maxwell Jacob Lerner and therefore the biological grandfather of Luke Skywalker Lerner.

3. Mr. Zhalovy is willing to take DNA tests to prove these statements.

A representative from this law firm will contact you within the next month to make offers from Mr. Zhalovy for each of you. In the meantime, feel free to call me or to consult with attorney of your own.

Respectfully,

Connie J. Evans

Connie J. Evans, Esq.
Attorney at Law

He used a female lawyer from the firm this time because he thought the women would be less put off by Connie than by either Isaac or David. He had a long conference with Connie in which they concluded that the first step in any reunion should be the simple letter that she sent out. She suggested to André that they give the women a week or ten days to digest the information and then Connie would call each individually to answer any questions they might have. After that, they would make a legal, written offer to each of them.

He wanted them to be his family. He wanted them to move to Oregon and live in his house and share his life. He knew deep down inside that he didn't deserve it, but he was unable to resist the need.

Just in case of a positive reaction, he hired a handyman named Henry, who lived around the area somewhere. Everyone knew Henry, but no one knew anything about him other than the fact that he was probably nearly sixty and that he was a little "simple." But he did good work and would work for ten dollars an hour.

Henry was an irascible old coot – well, he was a lot younger than André, but he just seemed older because he was so dimwitted. However, the things people said were true; Henry could and would do a lot of work and do it well. André offered to hire him full time because there was so much repair work to be done – things neglected for so long, but Henry wanted to just come by whenever he could "fit it in."

He didn't need a lot of direction. Henry just started in working and kept at it every time he came by – which was <u>almost</u> every day. He started with the yard, which was just a weed patch decorated with withered, dead plants. The trees were in good shape, but that's the nature of things in Oregon. Trees that are well established can make it with just the winter rains, whereas everything else will die off – except weeds.

Henry pulled or hoed the weeds – wouldn't touch weed killer spray. He said, "Bad…bad stuff…kill everything." He fertilized the soil (with natural cow manure, which he had André pick up at the farm store in town), and turned it, and watered it, and turned it again. He found a <u>lot</u> of daffodil bulbs, which he put into a big bucket in the shed to be replanted in the fall. When he figured the ground was ready, he went to the front door and knocked.

Cloud answered the door, "Yes, Henry, you need something? You want a glass of ice water? Or a beer?"

Henry took off his hat and tucked his chin down near his right shoulder so Cloud couldn't see his whole face, "Yes, Mam. I mean, no, Mam. Well, I don't drink beer. That's bad stuff. But ice water. Yes, Mam. And I need ta talk to Mr. André."

"Okay, just a minute, Henry. Don't go away."

"I won't."

Shortly, Cloud came back with a tall glass of ice water, which Henry drank in one long guzzling motion. So she went to fill it again. Meanwhile, André came down from his studio on the second floor and met Henry at the door.

"Whatcha need, Henry, old man?"

Henry jumped a little, having expected the man to come out of the door instead of down the outside steps. "Well, Mr. André," he said with his head bowed a little again, "I think I'm 'bout ready to plant for ya, but I don't know whatcha want me to plant."

"Oh, I see. Well, Henry, I actually hadn't thought about that. How about you and I take a ride down to the nursery and see what we like and what would go where?"

"I know some things kin go in the sun and some not – but I don't know which is which."

"That's all right, Henry. They'll be able to help us down at the nursery."

André let Henry into the passenger side of the Escalade and away they drove to town. André asked him if he lived close by, but Henry didn't answer. He just sat there with his white-knuckled hand clutching the door handle.

"I ain't never rode this fast before," Henry finally said, "and I allow as how I don't precisely like it."

"Sorry," André said and slowed down a little bit until they arrived at the nursery on the outskirts of town. "Let's have a look around, shall we?"

They walked around looking here and there – neither one of them knowing what they were looking for. Shortly, a young woman came out of the storefront and walked up to them in the nursery yard.

"Something I can do for you?" she asked.

"Well, hello there," André answered. "Yes, we have a lot of planting to do, and we have no idea what we want to plant."

Henry said, "I know some of the plants kin go in the sun and some not, but I don't rightly know which is which. I have a lot of space in the sun and a little space in the shade."

"All right, let's see. Did you want trees or bushes or flowers or what?" the girl asked.

"No trees," Henry answered, "We got trees aplenty."

André said, "Maybe a few little bushes – things that won't die over the winter – and lots of flowers. I want a lot of color. Maybe you can pick things out for us?"

So the girl got a couple of big carts. She pushed one, and Henry pushed the other. She described each item as she loaded it on the cart so that Henry could divide things up between sun and shade. They got hydrangea, lilies, violets, impatiens, pansies, and hosta for the shady areas. And they got dwarf bamboo, burning bush, several species of roses, kinnikinnick, rose of Sharon, geraniums, petunias, snapdragons, marigolds, daisies, day lilies, foxglove, rock roses, and nasturtiums for the sunny area. They got more than they could take home in one load, and had to go back for the rest.

When asked, Henry allowed, "Yup, I kin plant everythin' without any help."

While they were in town, André and Henry stopped at the hardware store and picked up all the pieces necessary for building a drip system to keep the flowers and bushes properly watered. The man at the store described exactly how Henry should put everything together. It would be a big job for Henry.

"'Course I'm up to it!" he answered crossly when asked. "I kin keep everthin' watered by hand until it's time to plant and turn on them little watering doodads."

Before long, they had lavender, white, purple, green, red, rose, pink, yellow, orange, blue and everything in between blossoming beside a green lawn and between the already well-established trees: Douglas fir, Ponderosa pine, dogwood, madrone, myrtle, incense cedar, chinkapin, oak, and several kinds of maple.

5. Mary Kathryn/Miki

"I left my h-e-a-r-t in San Fran-cis-co..." she sang with gusto as she used an already damp rag to clear the fog from the inside of the windshield even as the poor car's wipers struggled back and forth trying to throw the heavy rain off the glass. It was never a treat driving home from work, but when it rained in Southern California, the people seemed to go crazy. It appeared that if it rained, you drove as fast as you could to get out of it sooner **or** you drove as slow as you could to be super careful. It was a night like this when Miki avoided the 405 Freeway and took Sepulveda Boulevard all the way to the valley. Even so the water on the road had been treacherous in places with her near-bald tires, and the heater and defogger didn't work anymore – not to mention the radio.

"I really must get a new car," she said to herself and then quickly added, "Don't listen little car. I don't mean it; I love you. Please keep going."

Miki was in her 22nd year of teaching mathematics in the greater Los Angeles school district. Things were so different now than they had been when she started...fresh out of UC Santa Barbara and looking forward to teaching, and influencing, and forming young lives. She sometimes thought that she spent more time now with meetings and conferences and problem resolution than she did in the classroom. And she was tired. No, she was exhausted. Even the school administration no longer really supported the teachers. Chances were good that a teacher would be assaulted or raped – or accused of some ungodly or illegal act, against which there was little defense.

Teaching was no longer attractive. There were so many students who didn't even pretend to do homework or to take tests. Many told her point blank that they "didn't have to" and she "couldn't make them" do anything they didn't want to do. Holy cow! Would the world ever come to its senses and cease letting the inmates run the asylum?

Miki was so thankful that she had a cute little house and roommates to come home to, or she might just give it all up! She drove into the driveway and breathed a sigh of relief as she looked at the sweet little flower bordered house that she shared with her two housemates and all of the precious "children." They had Denzel, Dodger, and Punkin – a gorgeous young black Lab, a

yappy little dachshund, and a sweet gold and white Shih Tzu who had come from the shelter. "Imagine giving up a dog like that!" she thought ... not for the first time.

The dogs all bounded across the yard to greet Miki. Denzel wagged his entire body…starting from his heavy black tail and undulating all the way up to his head with his feet trying to keep up. He was young and gorgeous and black. That's how he got the Denzel name. And little Dodger dog – yipping and yapping as any dachshund would … followed by a happy, fluffy fur-ball. Miki scooped up Punkin to receive her welcome home kisses as she patted the other dogs.  What a delight to be so welcome every day – like everyday is Christmas or the 4th of July!

Miki and the kids walked through the garden and into the kitchen where Jake and Alan were stirring up something wonderful for dinner. This was the very best part of having roommates – they liked to cook and they did it very well. Tonight was something Italian – aromas of basil, oregano, and garlic were a dead giveaway along with the red wine already sitting on the table. Miki stripped out of her wet coat and shoes and grabbed a glass of the wine.

Jake handed Miki an envelope from the mail. "It's addressed to 'Mary Kathryn Miller.' I guess that must be you, Miki."

Miki looked at the creamy envelope and felt the embossed return address – lawyers in Portland, Oregon. She kept rubbing the embossing while she tried to think of what lawyers could be writing to her about.

Alan looked at her and said, "It's easier to read if you open it, you know."

Miki sat down and ran the envelope back and forth through her hands. Finally, she picked up a sharp kitchen knife and slit it open. She read it through once quickly and then again more slowly. All the while, Jake and Alan stood nearby, petting the dogs and trying not to appear inquisitive. Finally, Jake could stand the silence no longer.

"Well, what's up?"

"My father. It's my father," Miki said.

"Yes, well…what?"

"I never knew him, you know. All I ever knew was that my mother had his name put on the birth certificate: Andrew H. Miller. That's all I ever knew. Besides, I thought he was dead. Didn't I read that he was dead?" Miki asked and looked back and forth from Alan to Jake.

"Who? Who's dead?"

"André Zhalovy. He says he's my father, but I thought he was dead. Maybe my mother said he was dead. I'll have to ask her," Miki said absently as she continually stroked and folded and unfolded the letter.

"Okay, I give up. What are you talking about? André Zhalovy is very famous and rich … and not yet dead. How could he be your father?" Jake sat down next to Miki and patted her hand.

"Holy cow! I hardly know what to say … see, my mother met this guy when she was very young. He was so dashing and handsome and powerful, she said. No one could blame her really … well, no one but Grandma and Grandpa and the entire Catholic Church. The Grands, well they were nearly hysterical when they found out and wanted her to put me up for adoption." Miki paused, "But, you know, I think she really loved him. Things were always very secretive. We never talked about stuff, and I didn't even know Grandma and Grandpa weren't my real mom and dad until I was ten years old and saw my birth certificate with my mother listed as Mary Margaret Griffith and my father as Andrew Higgins Miller."

"But Miki, Jesus! Wake up. What if André Zhalovy is your dad? Aye caramba!" Jake got up and danced with Alan all around the room. "So Whatcha gonna do?"

"Call my mother, I guess."

So she did. She called the convent and asked to speak to Sister Mary Emancipación. Miki thought back to when her Grandmother had finally told her that her mother had been so guilt-ridden and so shunned after her pregnancy and childbirth that she had begged and had been given a place in the convent. She felt a calling to be with Jesus and to help other girls in trouble. So her mother went through the training of being a novice and finally took her vows, selecting the religious name of Mary Emancipación because she wanted to emancipate troubled girls. All the while Mary had been raised by her grandparents, the Griffith's. Some people thought it strange that she had a different last name, but no one ever spoke about her circumstances until she herself demanded the knowledge when she was old enough for confirmation. That was when her grandmother finally showed her the birth certificate and told her that she was their granddaughter – not their daughter, and that her mother was a nun. Wow, that was a shock at the time, and now another shock – having a father. Well, for goodness sake, she thought, everyone has a father. I just never knew anything about mine.

Finally, her mother came on the line, "Yes?"

"Hi, Mama, this is Miki – well, you probably knew that or you wouldn't have come to the phone, right? Well, I have a problem … a really big problem, and I think you can help me."

Her mother asked, "What in the world is happening? What's wrong, Chiquita?"

"Oh, Mama, "I got a letter – a letter from some kind of a big deal lawyer in Portland, Oregon, saying that my father is André Zhalovy. They said he used to be Andrew Miller and is now known as André Zhalovy – the famous author, you know. I just don't know what to think. Is it possible, Mama, or is it some sort of scam, do you think?"

"Oh, pobrecita, lo siento," her mother said softly.

"Please speak English, Mama. I'm not one of your East L.A. charity cases," Miki responded.

"I'm sorry. I'm sorry," the Sister/Mama said. "I just hoped never to hear that name again in my life, and I prayed that you would never hear it either."

"Was he that bad?" Miki asked.

"No. No…well, yes, maybe. He was wonderful. He was so handsome, Miki, very tall, blond, tanned and charming. Yes, so charming. I was just a child, you know. I had just turned eighteen and hadn't yet graduated from high school – Sacred Heart High School, you know."

"Yes, Mama, I know."

"Well, I met him. How did I meet him? Oh, it's so hard to remember things that you have purposely removed from your active memory and stored away someplace where it's hard to get at."

She paused, "Yes, I remember now, I met him at a friend's house. Caroline's mother was a customer at Andrew's gym and had invited him over for some reason. He offered me a ride home. He told me I was beautiful – that I looked like Ava Gardner. He asked if he could take me out for dinner sometime, and I told him 'No, my mother and father would never allow me to go out with an older man.' So he asked if he could give me a ride home from school sometimes and just stop for a coke or a shake or something.

"Oh, Madre Maria! My deep down little voice told me this would lead to no good, but I didn't listen. I couldn't listen. I was madly in love with him. Andrew was like an Apollo – he was golden. And I thought he loved me, too, but as soon as I told him I thought I was pregnant, he disappeared. I never saw him again. He broke my heart. He nearly broke my soul. He taught me a lot."

"Mama," Miki said softly, "I am so sorry. I didn't realize how much it would hurt you to talk about this. Please forgive me for asking but do you think that Andrew Miller could possibly be André Zhalovy?"

"Yes, I know that he is. I've seen his picture on the back of his books. He is older, of course. He is no longer the golden one, but he is the same man."

"Thank you, Mama. I love you."

"Oh, Chiquita, I love you, too. I always have and always will. But please be very careful about this man. He is not a good man."

I shared the information with Alan and Jake who were thrilled and immediately shared a toast to their "newly rich roommate."

I told them, "Don't get excited, fellas. The letter doesn't say much – doesn't say what he really wants from me. Let's just go on with life until I hear from the Portland lawyers again."

6. Joy

When her copy of the letter from Portland arrived, Joy was sitting at her desk on the 15th floor of the bank building, continuing the irksome task of correcting the uniformity of her PowerPoint presentation. Some people might have called it fussy, but Joy liked her presentations to flow from slide to slide with seamless precision, and that would not happen if some of the bullet points were aligned differently than others and if there were no spaces in front of some of the ellipses.

Joy's assistant, Rhonda, tapped at the door to announce the arrival of a special delivery envelope, and Joy barely nodded as she saw it dropped on her desk. It was, after all, Rhonda's fault that Joy was still working on this. It should have been done correctly in the first place.

"Oh well," Joy sighed, thinking that she would have to do something about Rhonda. Rhonda was in love, and a woman in love was really lousy with details. That's the problem with hiring young women … some sort of emotional trauma almost all the time. Joy was proud that at her age of fifty-one, she no longer had much interest in men. Well, and why would she? She'd had three marriages and the only good that came of those were two wonderful children, Michelle and Michael, both from the first marriage to Gregory Aiello … dark, passionate, Italian Gregory. Even after the other two short marriages to Philip and Mark, Joy had kept the Aiello name so that it would be the same as the children (until Michelle married that dolt, Steven). The Italian name was also a good ice breaker. People were instantly surprised to meet a tiny, olive-eyed, distinctly Chinese lady with an Italian surname.

Joy smiled at that thought and reached across the desk, picked up the envelope, and studied the return address from Weber, Stevens & Evans, Attorneys at Law. "Oh gawd!" she cried out loud. What now? Not another lawsuit involving the bank and involving her as a witness.

She tore open the envelope and scanned the letter. Then she adjusted herself in her chair, took a gulp of tepid coffee, and wished desperately that she could smoke in the building before she carefully read the letter again.

At the offset it was incredible. All she knew about her father was that his name was Andrew Miller and that he'd met her mother, Daisy Dxiang-Lee, when she won the Miss Chinatown contest. He was a friend of one of the judges or something. Her mother became pregnant right away and was unable to complete her year-long reign as Miss Chinatown – not to mention the loss of face for the entire Dxiang-Lee family.

"Oh my gawd!" she said again as she speed dialed her son's office phone. Michael was a young attorney in his dad's firm, doing well, married to a nice Chinese girl, and the father of a fine baby boy named Norman Zhang Aiello.

"Hello, Mom. Every okay?" Michael always checked the caller identity before picking up and his mother always got immediate attention.

"I need to talk, Michael. I've had a shock. A terrible shock – a letter from an attorney which says that my father is André Zhalovy," Joy said.

"You mean <u>the</u> André Zhalovy?" Michael queried.

"That's right. The name on my birth certificate was Andrew Miller. Apparently, somewhere along the way he changed his name. I never would have guessed. Mommie said he was tall, blond, and handsome – but, well, I've looked at André Zhalovy's picture on the backs of his books for years and never saw any resemblance or felt any connection…you know what I mean?"

"Gee, yes, Mom. This is incredible. Well, what does he want? What else did the letter say?"

"I'll fax it over to you so you can see it," Joy said, "but it really doesn't say much except to expect a call from the law firm in the near future."

"I'll look it over when I get it," Michael said, "But, wow! André Zhalovy – whew – money! I'll call you back after I look at the fax."

Joy sat there staring out the window at the Transamerica Tower and the Embarcadero Buildings – but not really seeing them. She was thinking about the

years she'd spent working to get to this 15th floor office and these windows. She thought about all the people who believed she'd slept her way to the top – Ha! She could have. Maybe she would have, but she didn't need to. She was good – very good at what she did and people listened when she talked. Good grief, she thought, this better not screw that up!

Her private line rang, and she picked it up with, "Well, what do you think?"

Michael answered, "I think it may be the real deal. I know this firm up in Portland. They wouldn't mess with anything that wasn't on the up and up. Want me to call this Connie Evans person and dig up some information for you?"

"Oh, yes, could you do that – please? I'm just a wreck from thinking about this," Joy said. "Oh, and if I don't answer when you call back, leave a message. I have to get a cigarette before I simply die!"

With that, Joy picked up her large black leather handbag and headed for the elevator, which she took to the roof. There was a wind-protected garden up there for smokers – no smoking at all in the building. In fact, according to the city ordinance, there wasn't supposed to be any smoking in public anywhere in the City. But who would know if one person lit up on the roof of the fifty-two story building? And if they did – well, screw 'em!

The blessing of the roof garden was also that it was usually above the fog of the City. It was fun to sit up there for a smoke or for lunch and look down on the fluffy top of the fog with just a few of the taller buildings jutting through. Only the really **big** kahunas got to look out of fog free windows most of the year in San Francisco. It might have been windy up so high, but there were natural wind breaks behind the air conditioning units plus the built-in breaks that the bank had "kindly" provided.

Joy sat at one of the tables and lit up her cigarette. She enjoyed smoking – at least that's what she told herself. And she had no intention of giving it up. It kept her calm while the caffeine was keeping her sharp. Besides, it was also keeping her thin. Most women her age had already spread a couple of sizes. Joy didn't want that to happen to her. Anyway, she didn't smoke that much – maybe a pack a day all together because of not being able to smoke at work or in a restaurant or just about anywhere except in her own car and in her own condo. She wondered – not for the first time – how long it would be before they banned smoking in her building. "Why can't people just mind their own business and stay out of mine," she thought as she ground out the stub of her smoke and went back down the elevator.

Her message light was blinking, and she called Michael right away. "Well?" she said.

"No soap. This Ms. Evans, as she likes to be called, wouldn't give out a peep of information about André Zhalovy and what he might be up to, but she did say that she would definitely call you within the next couple of days. She said that if I'd seen the first letter, I knew what there was to know at the moment. She also said that it was nothing to worry over. So that's all the news I have from this end. Sorry."

"Okay, I guess, I'll just have to wait – although maybe I could try to Google the other people on that list and see if I can find out what they know."

"Well, I don't see how it could hurt. Go ahead, but don't be upset if you don't find them. I'll talk to you at home tonight. Love you."

"Love you, too."

She immediately went to Google search and looked up Deirdre Lerner – and found nothing much other than some other Lerners in other areas. She was pretty sure that they weren't relatives. Then, she entered Mary Kathryn Miller and got thousands of hits, but none of them were in the Burbank or Los Angeles area.

"Crap!" she said out loud. She figured that she might as well go home early and have a drink to settle her down.

7. Deirdre/Dolly

The year had been, in general, lousy. Well, there were some up moments but average those together with the really devastating bits and you come up with lousy, horrible, crummy.

Dolly (Deirdre Townsend) and Max (Maxwell Jacob Lerner) had met while they were both students at Humboldt State University in Arcata, California, studying forestry. They had been great buddies in college – helping each other with homework. He was best at all things involving English and literature, and she was superior in chemistry and math. He also taught her to drink beer, and she taught him to ski (cross-country and downhill) and rock climb. So they made a good pair.

It just sort of seemed natural for them to get married once they graduated. They both applied with the U.S. Forest Service, and both got hired on as interns at the Yreka office. In the course of the additional training, they learned about fighting wildfires and that they could make a lot of additional money by signing up to do that in the summers.

Dolly gave up the firefighting part of her job when she found out she was pregnant. She didn't want to take any chances with her precious cargo. So Max took up smoke jumping for an even greater bump in the annual income. The fires were scary enough in and of themselves, but Dolly was constantly worried whenever

Max went off to the Boise headquarters and prepared to join with other smoke jumpers to go to fires all over the Western U.S.

The baby, Luke, was almost a year old when Max was injured on one of his jumps. Dolly thanked whatever gods had saved his life in the midst of the Hell of the fire, but the injury was bad enough. It had required several surgeries and a back brace at all times. Max was in constant pain. He took Vicodin to relieve the pain and settled into a desk job at the office. In fact, they both took desk jobs so that Dolly could have flex hours and spend more time with Luke while he was little. When he was born, Max wanted very much to name him Luke Skywalker Lerner. Dolly protested that the poor kid would be teased all his life, but Max won out by assuring her that most people never even knew anyone else's middle name.

The time came for Max when the Vicodin no longer helped him with the pain. His doctor prescribed Oxycontin, and Max felt much better – for a long time – but he began to drink to supplement the pain killer. At first it was just an occasional beer, and Dolly didn't worry too much about that (though maybe she should have). Soon it was a shot of whiskey and a couple of beers a night. But before long, Dolly had to admit that she had no idea how much liquor and how many drugs Max was using. He was getting more and more secretive and would react violently when she questioned him. Oh, he never hit her or anything like that, but he shouted, scared the baby, threw things, stomped around, and left the house.

Dolly was worried. She talked to Max's doctor, and the doctor said he would talk to Max about the problem. However, that backfired when paranoid Max accused her of "setting him up" with the doctor – and would she please stay out of his business! He now had drugs that she didn't recognize and bottles hidden here and there in strange places around the house. She had no idea what to do.

She talked to her family. She talked to his mother. But no one really believed that he had a serious problem. She was just blowing it all out of proportion – after all, "he did go to work every day, didn't he?" And she had to admit that he did – but he just wasn't Max any more. He was someone else. He was someone secretive, fearful, and suspicious. He lied a lot and ate very little. He began to steal money from Dolly's purse, and he spent more and more time alone – never going near the baby or Dolly.

The day finally came when Dolly got a visit from the Yreka Police who wanted her to sit down please and then went on, "Mrs. Lerner, I am very sorry to have to bring you this news, but your husband, Maxwell, has been found dead of an apparent drug overdose. I am truly sorry for your loss."

Dolly repeated in her head: "I am truly sorry for your loss." It echoed there ("I am truly sorry for your loss"), but it didn't seem to reach her somehow. It was intangible. It was something she couldn't get her head around. But she finally asked, "Where? When? Oh god! Can I see him?"

"Yes, Mam, I'll take you downtown. You're needed to identify the body. We found him early this morning in the park. We thought he was asleep under a tree, but we found that he had no pulse and had been dead for some time."

Dolly moved as if she were swimming through Jell-O as she went to get the baby, a blanket, the diaper bag, and a jacket. She looked around and around, thinking that she was forgetting something, but she couldn't decide what it was. So she let the policeman lead her out of the house and deposit Luke and her in the patrol for the ride to the Siskiyou County Courthouse.

A policewoman took the baby and promised to take good care of him as Dolly was led to a viewing window. She looked down at her feet as they opened the blinds that blocked the window. Slowly she looked up at the grayish-white body covered except for the face with an even whiter sheet. It was a sight that burned itself into her brain. It was her husband. It was Max, but really it was only a cold, antiseptic piece of meat that used to be Max.

The policeman asked her, "Is this your husband, Maxwell Lerner?"

Dolly nodded and answered, "Yes, it is."

And that was that – or at least that was the start of that. She had to call her mother-in-law. She had to call her family. She had to make funeral plans. She had to call her supervisor. She had to get out of there!

She thanked the nice policewoman for taking care of Luke who was now only old enough to walk and not anything near old enough to understand that Daddy was gone and was never coming back.

The policewoman asked if there was anyone she could call. Dolly thought about that and finally said, "Yes, would you please call my friend, Sherry. She's at work at the Forest Service. Her number is 555-9876."

Sherry got to the police station very quickly. Dolly couldn't believe that any time had passed at all. She'd just been talking to the policewoman. Then she sat down with Luke, and then Sherry was there. Sherry's car was right outside, and they drove slowly and silently back to Dolly's house.

Sherry took Luke from her and told Dolly to sit down while she changed Luke's diaper and then she'd get them something to drink. A moment later (or so it seemed), she was back with two glasses of sweetened iced tea, which was what she knew Dolly preferred. Sherry sat down next to Dolly and held her hand. Then she drew closer to her…and hugged her…and held her tightly while she broke down and sobbed – wept until she had no more tears.

Thinking back on it now all these years later, she realized that Sherry had been her rock – as had all the folks at the Forest Service. They all came to Max's service, along with all of Dolly's family and Max's mother, Dorothy Lerner. It was a beautiful service – though Dolly didn't understand a lot of it because she wasn't Jewish and had never learned anything about Max's faith because he never talked about it. Dorothy had been good enough to make all the arrangements so Dolly didn't have to think about what would be appropriate. She did give Dolly the ashes – which the forest service flew up and spread on the wind over the Toiyabe National Forest. It was where he would have wanted to be.

But this day at her desk as the GIS (Geographical Information Systems) Administrator, she received a letter that took her completely by surprise. All mail coming into the Federal facility had to be opened and examined before delivery to the addressee, so it wouldn't be long before everyone in the building knew what it said. Many of them didn't know that her name was Deirdre, but she was definitely the only Lerner around. She could already hear some buzzing of the name Zhalovy.

She wasn't really sure of what this new development in her life would mean, but she was sure that Luke needed to know about it. Luke, who had just been walking when his daddy died, was now a big twelve year old computer buff and natural athlete – baseball, football, basketball – any old ball – and even track…the high hurdles and the relay races. She knew that there was a chance that she was slightly prejudiced,

 but she thought that Luke was truly and extraordinary young man. But she worried, too. She worried because Dorothy had thought Max was extraordinary and Dolly agreed – and then look what happened to him.

After work that day, she picked Luke up from baseball practice and offered to take him out for a burger and fries. This was completely unexpected and unlike his mother who always badgered him about eating healthy.

He asked, "Why? What's up? Did I do something wrong?"

"No," Dolly answered, "I just want to sit down someplace with you and have a little talk."

"Oh no! Not the birds and bees talk again," Luke laughed, "I saw the movie, Mom."

"Just trust me. Okay?"

They drove to the local Burger King, placed their order, and sat across from each other – both unwrapping their cheeseburgers and sipping chocolate shakes. Finally, Luke couldn't stand it any more and said, "Okay, what's the big deal? What are we doing here?"

And she told him about the letter and all the ramifications of it – it meant that Luke's father wasn't really a Lerner – it meant…well, she wasn't sure what all it meant, but she thought he should know about it.

"And so now we wait until we hear from the lawyers again?" Luke asked.

"Yes, we wait."

8. Decisions ... Decisions ... Decisions

Good to her word, Connie Evans, the Portland attorney, did call Joy first. Two days after the letter from Weber, Stevens & Evans, P.C. had arrived, Joy received a call from Ms. Evans outlining the arrangement that Mr. Zhalovy wished to make with each of this children.

She stated, "Mr. Zhalovy is completely willing to have a DNA test made if you are unsure of his position as your biological father."

"No," Joy answered, "I'm fairly sure from my own investigations that he is telling the truth about that. So what does he want from me now after all these years?"

The lawyer responded, "Mr. Zhalovy lives quite alone – except for a housekeeper – on a large piece of property in Oregon. He would like to offer you the opportunity to live there with all of your expenses paid until the occasion of his death at which time you would inherit your portion of the estate. The single portions depend entirely on how many of his progeny are willing to move there and how many stay once there."

"Why? What's wrong with the place?"

"Nothing. I assure you, Mrs. Aiello, the estate is quite lovely and extensive. The house has six bedrooms and seven bathrooms – all quite private. The grounds are lovely with a wide lawn, many flowers, and a forested area. Mr. Zhalovy would be very pleased to pay your expenses to visit, and if you decide not to stay, that would be your decision alone."

"How soon do I have to decide?" Joy asked.

"Mr. Zhalovy would like to have you all there before the summer is over so that you would not have to contend with any possible snow or ice on the roads. The weather is generally very mild in southwestern Oregon where he lives, but there are those rare occasions when a winter storm will blow in," Ms. Evans told her.

"Should I call you back? Or what do I do at this point?"

"Yes, please call me as soon as you have made a decision and I will make all the arrangements for you. You have my number, I believe, but if not it is 503-555-7634. Please just tell my secretary who you are, and she will put you through directly. And thank you very much for taking time to talk with me."

Joy sat there thinking and wishing for a cigarette and called Michael. He was in court – so she left a message that she had news – maybe sort of good news – maybe really good news!

She forwarded her private line to her cell phone and went up the elevator to the roof shelter for a smoke. She really needed a hit of nicotine. But what she really needed was time to think things over without the interruption of the phone or that little irritating voice announcing: "You have a message."

This was an exceptional day – no fog. No fog in San Francisco in June was like Christmas! People went around in short-sleeved shirts – swearing it must be eighty degrees! Whew! Well, anyway, Joy looked out on the City. She loved it. It was a beautiful place – if you didn't look too closely. Actually, the City had gotten to be the crime, grime, and illegal alien capital of northern California. *Wait a minute ... you couldn't call them illegal aliens anymore, could you? What was the current politically correct designation anyway? She couldn't remember.* At any rate, it wasn't safe to go out at night anymore like it once was. Sometimes it wasn't even safe to go out in the daytime. She hated the stinky, ugly homeless beggars and the rats as big as chihuahuas that she often saw if she walked to a meeting or to lunch. Of course, she drove to work. It wasn't far, but the parking was one of her job perks so she felt like she had to use the space marked: "**Joy Dxiang Aiello, Vice President**," And besides, her Mercedes was a dream to drive – another luxury of her current life. On the other hand, she thought, wouldn't it be nice to live worry-free. Imagine not having to get up with an alarm clock anymore. Imagine not having to attend meetings every day – endless meetings with so little purpose. Imagine not having to wear high-heeled shoes and pantyhose everyday! Imagine doing whatever she wanted to do everyday...*wait a minute...what in the world would she do if she didn't work everyday? She didn't have any hobbies. She just worked – always had.*

Just about then, her cell phone rang. It was Michael, "What's up, Mom?"

"I finally heard from the lawyers again. It seems that Mr. Zhalovy wants his 'children' to move up to his estate in Oregon – all expenses paid and live there with him ... I suppose to create some sort of family for himself. The deal is that when he dies, his estate will be divided between those of us who move up there and stay up there with him."

"Gee, Mom, that sounds like a really good deal. All expenses paid, huh?" Michael asked.

"That's what she said. I asked her why and what was wrong with the place, and she assured me that it is a lovely, big place and that Mr. Zhalovy is entirely serious about this."

"Well, what are you thinking of doing?"

"I don't know. I hate to give up what I have here. I finally got the job I want and the office I want with two windows."

"Yeah, Mom, but you know how you hate all the office politics and the younger women coming quickly up the ladder pushing you and pushing you. You grumble about them to me all the time."

Joy sighed, "Yes, I suppose I do. Sorry."

"No, I'm not complaining. I just want you to look at this from all angles. When do you have to decide?"

"Well, she said that Mr. Zhalovy wants us all up there before the end of the summer – just in case there is a sudden change in the weather or something. I'm supposed to call her back as soon as I decide. What would you do?" Joy queried.

"Good grief, Mom, I'd go. I'd go in a 'New York minute!' You can have a lovely time and do whatever you want to do."

"And, Michael, that begs the question – what would I do? I've never done anything other than work. I don't have hobbies. I don't know how to do the little tricky things that other women do in their spare time."

Michael thought a minute and answered, "Well, you could learn something – like photography or sewing or art. He's an artist, isn't he? Maybe you could learn from him. Don't let that little complication stop you. Just think about it … and let me know what you decide. I'm behind you all the way."

Dolly got her phone call at work the same day. It was difficult to talk much at work, but the lawyer worked the same hours she did – so it was that or nothing, she guessed. And she was so happy to get on with this and stop imagining all sorts of complications for a possible custody battle for Luke. This was the worst thing she'd thought of and couldn't get it out of her mind.

The lawyer started with, "Mr. Zhalovy is completely willing to have a DNA test made if you are unsure of his position as your late husband's biological father and therefore grandfather of your son."

"No," Dolly said, "I'm pretty sure that isn't necessary. I just want to know what he wants with me and with my son."

Ms. Evans responded, "Mr. Zhalovy lives quite alone – except for a housekeeper – on a large piece of property in Oregon. He would like to offer you and your son the opportunity to live there with all of your expenses paid until the occasion of his death at which time your son would inherit his portion of the bequests. The single portions depend entirely on how many of you are willing to move there and how many stay once there."

"All expenses? Even medical care and educational expenses or whatever for my son?" Dolly asked.

"Yes, Mr. Zhalovy was quite explicit that all expenses would be taken care of, and that your son would receive a superior education…if that's what he wants."

"And what does he want from me. What's the catch?"

"I assure you, Mrs. Lerner, there is no 'catch' that I am aware of. Mr. Zhalovy has a large, beautiful estate. He lives essentially alone. He is lonely. He wants to have a family, and he wants to make up in some small way for neglecting his children for all these years. If you elect to go to Oregon, I will meet you there with the legal papers to be signed so that these promises will be enforceable and proper."

"How soon do I have to decide?"

"Mr. Zhalovy would like to have all of you there before the end of the summer – actually the sooner the better as far as your son is concerned so that he can be enrolled in school or have a tutor or whatever is necessary. I'd like you to think this over and let me know as soon as you can."

Dolly sighed heavily, and said, "Okay, I'll talk with my son and see what he wants to do. We'll kick it around a little. I have your number. I'll call you as soon as I can."

"Thank you for your time, Mrs. Lerner."

Dolly leaned back in her chair, tossing all these thoughts around in her head. All expenses, huh? God, it would be good to get away from working for the government. The Forest Service was now bound by so many legal chains that much of the time, they weren't doing anything. At least half of all the foresters had been laid off. No one was managing the forests because the eco-whackos kept taking them to court. They couldn't thin. They couldn't fertilize. They couldn't spray herbicide. They couldn't clear snags and burns. It was a mess, and she was so tired of fighting the war between the people who knew what was right for the forest (the scientists/foresters) and the people who just wanted everything to be "virgin and natural" (the eco-whackos). She often wondered what would happen if one of them actually had to go live in the "virgin and natural" world.

But Dolly knew that the decision about Oregon really had to come from Luke. He was the one who would have to change schools and move away from his friends and his grandparents, and that reminded her, too, that maybe she should consult Dorothy. Well, she'd ask Luke.

That evening she and Luke sat down and talked about the whole situation and the decision that would need to be made. At first Luke was completely against moving. He liked his friends. He liked his school where he was "big man on campus." But the more they talked about being out in the woods and that his mother wouldn't have to work but could do whatever she wanted to do, the more Luke started to come around. He thought maybe he could even have a dog. Maybe?

Dolly told him that they needed to decide as soon as possible because she would have to give a minimum of two weeks notice on her job, though a month would be better. GIS specialists were still rare individuals, and the job might be hard to fill. They both agreed to think things through carefully and talk again in a couple of days.

Miki was at home when her call came. School was out and she was out in the yard with the dogs, weeding the flower beds and giving them a little boost of Miracle Gro. She loved working in the garden. Just getting her hands into the dirt was relaxing somehow. What she didn't enjoy was the heat of the day, and it was time she went in to the air-conditioned house – just then the phone rang.

Miki ran in, picked up the phone, and quickly said, "Yes, this is Miki but I've got mud all over my hands. Please hold on just a sec while I wash off."

When she got back to the phone and wiped the mud off, she apologized, "I'm sorry to keep you waiting. This is Miki, what can I do for you?"

It was the lawyer, "Hello, Mary Kathryn, or do you prefer Miki? This is Ms. Evans of Weber, Stevens & Evans."

"Oh, hello. Oh, yes, I prefer Miki, but you can call me any old thing – my students certainly do."

Ms. Evans laughed lightly and said, "I can imagine what sort of a vocabulary a high school student has these days! Anyway, as you may have guessed, I've called you with the particulars of Mr. Zhalovy's offer."

"I can't wait to hear it."

"Mr. Zhalovy lives quite alone – except for a housekeeper – on a large estate in Oregon. He would like to offer you the opportunity to live there with all of your expenses paid until the occasion of his death at which time you would inherit your portion of the bequests. Each single portion depends entirely on how many of you are willing to move there and how many stay once there."

"Oh my goodness! Is it a nice place?" Miki asked.

"I have been there, and I can tell you that the estate is quite lovely and extensive. The house has six bedrooms and seven bathrooms – all quite private. The grounds are lovely with a wide lawn, many flowers, and a forested area. Mr. Zhalovy would be very pleased to pay your expenses to visit, and if you decide not to stay, that would be your decision alone."

"Can I bring my dogs?" Miki asked.

"Oh, I'm sure that wouldn't be a problem. Actually, the place is ideal for dogs – lots of room to run and have fun and maybe chase a rabbit or a squirrel."

"Okay, let me see…hmmmm…I guess I'd better ask what he wants from me? What's the catch? Is there a hidden snag that I should know about?" Miki asked timidly.

"Not at all. Mr. Zhalovy is quite serious. I think he's lonely. I think he wants to make up for past mistakes. And everyone wants to know how soon they have to decide. The answer to that is that he'd like to have you all there before the end of the summer to avoid any possible surprise weather changes which would make it so much more difficult all around."

"Well, my dear Ms. Evans, you don't need to wait for my answer. I've been teaching math to little hooligans for twenty-two years. I'm tired…no, I'm exhausted. My answer is a definite yes, and how soon can I get directions to his house?"

The lawyer laughed again and said, "He will be so pleased. I will send you a map to his house. It is out in the country and somewhat hard to find unless you've been there. Or I can make airline reservations for you and arrange to have you picked up and driven there. Which would you prefer?"

Mike answered, "I want to take my dogs, and I would never put them in the baggage compartment of an airplane. I'll drive…if my little old car will make it. I'll be ready to leave here in about a week. Can you get the map to me before that?"

"Absolutely. And I'll meet you there – if you'll call me with an exact date. Thanks so much, Ms. Miller."

9. Meanwhile, Back at the Ranch

André was, as Ms. Evans predicted, very pleased to know that Mary Kathryn Miller had readily agreed to come to Oregon. He was so energized that he even worked with Cloud and Henry to get one of the guest cottages ready. They agreed that with the two dogs she might like the feeling of being outside and away from the main house. Cloud cleaned and put freshly washed sheets, quilts, and towels in the little bungalow. She thought it was so cute – like a playhouse.

André went to town and bought all sorts of dog supplies – not realizing, of course, that Mary Kathryn would bring her own things for the dogs. He bought beds, toys, dishes, food, treats, toys, shampoo, collars, leashes, and toys. He was an instant favorite customer at Petco where he also picked up advice on when to bring the dogs in for grooming. He was not surprised to know that Labradors require very little grooming and love baths, but the other, the Shih Tzu, would require frequent grooming and probably did not enjoy baths.

Meanwhile, Miki had, of course, talked over her decision with her roommates, Alan and Jake. They would miss her, of course, but were anxious for her to go. They helped her pack up all her books, gadgets, school papers, and everything she would not need in Oregon. Alan and Jake agreed to (1) store Miki's stuff in a safe, water-free place; (2) keep the house and garden looking lovely and if they should ever sell it, to send her the portion of the equity that was hers; (3) let her take Denzel and Punkin as long as they could keep Dodger Dog *(people in Oregon don't know about our baseball team's Dodger Dogs they had said and Miki had to agree)*; and (4) to visit her in Oregon sometime.

She got her poor old Volvo serviced, and when she was ready, she called Ms. Evans to tell her that she would arrive in about two and a half days – because she didn't drive fast and because she intended to stop frequently and let the dogs out to play and "whatever." Thus, she had traveled from the 405 to the I-5 and then all the way up through the hot San Juaquin Valley of California where the majority of the country's food is grown. She had been singing things like "California Here I Come," and "I Left my Heart in San Francisco," "California Girls," and "California Dreamin'" along with Johnny Cash's "I Fell into a Burning Ring of Fire," Peggy Lee's "Fever," plus "Cool, Cool Water." She crossed the state line into Oregon and tried to think of a song to sing that featured Oregon – thinking of none, she sang "Follow the Yellow Brick Road" at the top of her lungs. She and the dogs liked the singing. Often Denzel would howl his tenor accompaniment for her.

Miki was pleased that the old Volvo was doing well. She went over the Siskiyou Summit with no problem and then faced several of the smaller summits as she drove along looking for a good place to stop for lunch and gasoline. She finally pulled off at Exit 119 and got gas and lunch at the truck stop there. She let the dogs loose to run in the neighbor's mowed and dried hay field. Denzel ran around and around while Punkin strolled along the edges where there were no sharp weeds to hurt her feet. What a couple they were! Miki gave them a dish of water and a small piece of doggie treat and loaded them back in the car for the remainder of the trip – which promised to be not all that far. She had only to go to Exit 138 – just another nineteen miles – and turn towards the ocean and then watch for the signs pointing their way to Daffodil Hill.

She hadn't reckoned for the twisty mountain roads after she turned off the freeway, and didn't like them a bit – except that the trees were magnificent, beautiful, wonderful – and the verdant undergrowth was something she'd never seen before. It was just green everywhere with sword ferns, rhododendrons, smaller trees of several kinds, and lots of things that Miki couldn't begin to identify. It was like being in a cathedral. It was captivating and sublime. And it was cool and dark. The dogs whined to get out.

She said to the dogs, "I sure hope the people who live with all this beauty know how lucky they are!"

Soon enough Miki found the sign for the Daffodil Hill turnoff all decorated with balloons so that it would have been hard to miss. She thought she would just turn in the driveway and there it would be – but again there was a long winding road leading up the hill – up and up. The graveled road ended in a big black-topped parking area in front of the impressive house and its beautiful garden.

Instantly, three people popped out of the front door to the house to greet the new arrivals. A young girl in shorts and tank top – very, very short hair and lots of piercings; a white-haired man in chinos and a short sleeved plaid shirt; and finally, a slender, mature woman in a pant suit and heels. The dogs bounded out of the car and ran around and between everyone, sniffed everyone and everything and immediately relieved themselves on the carpet of green grass.

André laughed and said, "Yes, you kids make yourselves at home. And hello to you Mary Kathryn. I am more than happy – I am ecstatic – to meet you at last."

"Please call me Miki. Yes, it's nice to meet you Mr. Zhalovy – though I don't exactly know yet how I feel about you and about the forty-seven years that I didn't know you."

"I understand. There is time – plenty of time."

"Hello, Miki, I am Connie Evans. We have talked on the phone several times, and I am also delighted to meet you. This is Cloud. She is Mr. Zhalovy's housekeeper."

Miki shook hands with both of the women and wondered how anybody got a name like "Cloud." So she asked, "How did you get a name like Cloud?"

"My mother. My mother was a sort of wannabe hippie. She named me Cloud and my brother is River. She is Nancy but likes to be called Petal."

After a pause, Cloud offered to carry Miki's baggage to the guest house – and Connie wanted her to come into the main house to look at the legal papers, because Connie wanted to start back for her flight from Eugene to Portland before it got dark. But when Miki opened the back of her car, it was clear that Cloud was going to need help with all the stuff that Miki had managed to cram inside of it. André stepped up and offered to help – and Miki went into the house with Connie to see the papers so that Connie wouldn't be held up any longer than necessary.

André made a face of disgust as he saw the beat-up Volvo that Miki had been driving, and murmured quotes of the bumper stickers that he saw all over the back of her car:

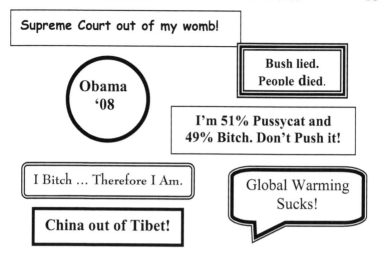

Connie and Miki entered the huge common room of the house, and Miki was very impressed with the size of it and the quality and taste of the furnishings. Obviously, Miki thought, these things were picked out by Mrs. Zhalovy before her death. They were not the rustic, country type of things that Miki had expected.

Connie sat down at the dining table and waved Miki to a seat. "This agreement between you and Mr. Zhalovy is already signed by him. You can take all the time you need before you sign it. Just be sure you date it and have it witnessed when you do sign it. The timing could turn out to be vital if Mr. Zhalovy passes away before you sign it. Basically, the agreement is simply that you agree to live here on Mr. Zhalovy's estate, which his late wife had called Daffodil Hill. And that you agree to stay until the time of his death or your own whichever comes first. All of your expenses will be paid, and you will receive a monthly allowance to do with as you see fit. At the time of Mr. Zhalovy's death the estate will be divided between those persons who have lived here during this period. And that's about it.

As I said, take time to read it. If you decide to stay, take it to the bank in town where they will witness your signature and forward the original papers to me with a copy to you and to André. If you decide, on the other hand, that you do not wish to stay, don't sign it. Just call me, and I'll make arrangements for you to be moved back to southern California or wherever you choose."

Miki glanced at the several pages of legalize in front of her, and said, "This is a lot to take in. I will read it, of course, but I'd like your personal word that there isn't anything tricky in here that you haven't told me about."

Connie smiled and patted Miki's hand, "Believe me, I would tell you if you needed to worry at all. The only thing that you have to worry about here is the total darkness at night because there is no civilization around and the complete quiet as well. Keep your dogs in at night. This is forest land, and there are animals around that would not make the dogs feel welcome."

"Oh, thank you, Connie, I hadn't thought of that. So I'd better go check on them now, and you can get on your way back to your flight. Thank you for all your help," Miki said and impulsively she pulled Connie to her and hugged her.

"You're a little scared. I can tell, but it will be all right. Cloud is here until after she cleans up after dinner, and I'm sure she'd show you around so you know where everything is. You'll like it. Wait and see."

Miki and Connie walked back outside. Connie got into her rental car and drove off down the road, waving as she went. Cloud and André met Miki and offered to show her where they had deposited her things and her dogs.

They walked back through the huge front doors and straight through the house to a sun porch which had three doors marked (by Cloud) North Star, Cassiopeia, and Southern Cross. They went through the door to the North Star guest house and followed a path through the trees that was completely covered by Plexiglas with steel supports. The guest house turned out to be a hexagonal cottage with the dogs waiting inside, looking out the window for their "mom."

Miki was enchanted with the little cottage. It was bigger than any bedroom space she'd ever had and featured a small kitchenette and a complete bathroom with a Jacuzzi tub. There was a skylight over the bed so she'd be able to look up at the sky while she was in bed. The interior was rustic in design but all of the curtains, towels, chair cushions, and bed coverings were her favorite color – a beautiful blue green.

"How could you have known my favorite color?" Miki asked. "This is beautiful. I love it."

"Oh, I am so glad," Cloud said, "I just guessed. I thought about your name and where you lived, and I just came up with aqua. I hope I do as well with the others."

"Are you expecting them soon?" Miki asked.

André answered, "Don't know yet. I think so, but nothing definite yet."

"Well, I hope they come. It will make for a nice family," Cloud said.

"Yes, I agree. And I'd really like to meet them. I have no brothers or sisters, you know," Miki said.

"Well, hopefully you will soon."

Miki offered to help Cloud with dinner, but Cloud and André insisted that Miki must be tired and she should get a little rest before dinner. Besides, Cloud declared, "You have a lot of stuff to find places for, and

André bought a lot of dog things. You'll find everything, I'm sure. I'll call you a little before dinnertime. Do you want to feed the dogs in here or in the kitchen?"

"Oh, I'll feed them right in here. This is perfect."

Walking back to the house, André commented, "God, she's fat – and plain. Her mother was so pretty and little. What the Hell happened?"

10. Sunshine, Lollipops, Nettles & Burrs

After a nice dinner with Cloud and André, Miki took the dogs for a walk (on leash) around the grounds so that they could relieve themselves before going to bed. The outside lights were on and the yard was well lighted, but it was so very quiet that Miki was a little spooked and glad to get back inside when the dogs were ready.

Connie had not exaggerated the totality of the darkness when Miki clicked all the lights off as she went to bed and someone in the house doused the lights there. Miki was glad to have her two "guards" with her. She had introduced them to their new beds, but they knew that the queen-sized bed would be softer, and nudging up to Miki would be warmer. So the three of them slept soundly together until Denzel woke her up barking at a bird that was sitting on their skylight.

It was time to get up anyway, and Miki was so glad that there was a bathroom and a coffee pot right there in her cottage. As soon as she could, she took the dogs out, but she decided that they might just as well run loose a little during the daytime.

Later in the day, Cloud helped her put together some lunchable supplies, including a large bag of cherries, a nice piece of Brie, French bread, a little bottle of white wine, and a sack of dog treats, and Miki took the dogs with her for a little walkabout plus lunch.

It was a beautiful day – blue sky with only a couple of tiny, puffy clouds just for set decoration. And Miki was singing again (as she often did), "Sunshine, lollipops and rainbows and everything that's wonderful is what I feel when we're together..."[iii]

After being satisfied that there was no more picnic food to beg for, the dogs ran around and around on the grass and then into the woods to hunt for lions, tigers, and bears, oh my! When they came back out of the woods, Denzel was carrying a stick in his mouth which he wanted tossed as far as Miki could throw it so that he could run after it and bring it back. He loved to play "fetch." However, today that would have to wait.

Punkin, bless her little Shih Tzu heart, came out of the woods looking like a bush. Her breed of dog has a double coat of hair that will pick up anything and hold onto it tenaciously. Though Punkin had been clipped in a "teddy bear" cut because she was not a show dog and truly hated the daily brushing that long hair required, her hair still picked up all sorts of seeds, brambles, thorns, nettles, and burrs. She was now so full of stuff that her natural imperial gait was more like a waddle as she stumbled back to the picnic blanket area.

Back at the cottage Miki tenderly tried to brush the trash out of Punkin's hair, but it was obvious that in spite of her care, it was hurting the poor little dog. Thus, Miki conferred with Cloud to find out about the nearest groomer. Cloud drove her to town so she wouldn't get lost, and poor little Punkin had most of her hair shaved off. She looked so forlorn and pitiful.

Afterwards Miki said to Cloud, "Poor baby. I named her Punkin because I thought she was such a cute little Punkin, and she has always acted as if she were proud. You know, she doesn't just walk around. She carries herself with a distinctly arrogant carriage. Fortunately, the groomer was able to save the long tail hair. I love her long tail and the way it curls up and over her back. But I hope this indignity will not affect her personality."

While they were downtown, they stopped at a little market so that Miki could pick up supplies that she needed: a nightlight for her cottage, two liters of Coke, a bag of potato chips, chocolate chip cookies, and a couple of Hershey® bars. Cloud told her that André would be disappointed that he had not provided everything she could possibly want – so Miki told her just forget to tell him about it.

Punkin was fine when she got home. She didn't know how she looked. As far as she was concerned, she was still the queen of everything and was glad to be back to see Denzel.

André knocked on Miki's cottage door in the middle of the afternoon and asked if he might come in and talk to her. Naturally, Miki invited him in.

André sat in the chair, and Miki sat on the bed with Denzel at her feet and Punkin on her lap. André cleared his throat and said, "So, um, tell me about yourself."

Miki paused and responded, "What do you want to know? I'm forty-seven years old. That's sort of a long story."

"Well, I mean, I know that you were a teacher for a long time. What did you teach? Where did you go to school? What do you like to do? Stuff like that."

"Okay," Miki said, "I taught Algebra, Geometry, and Trigonometry for twenty-two years to a bunch of kids in East L.A. At first it was great. The kids listened. I taught. I helped. I thought I made a difference in some of their lives. But as time went on, especially the last ten or so years, it was a real struggle. The kids didn't listen. They didn't want to learn. They didn't want to be there – and their parents (for the most part) didn't care. It was a losing battle because the administration would not stand up for the teachers, and none of the students were to be allowed to fail. Everyone had to pass the class – or there was something wrong with the teacher, you know? And I went to school at UC Santa Barabara. It was a lovely school. I have always loved math – especially Algebra, which is like solving puzzles or little mysteries – but the school didn't prepare any of us for life. It prepared us for Utopia, which, of course, doesn't exist."

"How interesting," André said, "you have had quite a time. Have you never married?"

"No. I never wanted to. I like being on my own. I did have two roommates in our house in Northridge – a couple of wonderful gay guys who kept the "man" stuff done for me – like cleaning out the rain gutters, checking the air in my tires, and killing bugs. Oh, and they also opened jars for me. Other than that, I never felt the need for a man of my own."

"You had gay roommates?" André asked.

"Yes," Miki responded, waiting for the next remark.

"So are you a Lesbian?"

Miki laughed and answered, "See, I knew you were going to ask that! And, you know what? It's none of your business."

"Hmmm … So how's your mother. She was such a doll. Whatever became of her?"

"Oh God! I really think that's none of your business as well – but I'll tell you what happened if you'll just sit there and listen and not interrupt."

"Sure."

"Okay, here goes…you ruined my mother's life…quite literally. I was born, my grandparents adopted me – except they gave me the last name of Miller because that's what Mother had listed on my birth certificate. 'Father: Andrew Higgins Miller.' My mother went away, and I didn't know until I was ten years old that Mama and Papa were actually my Grandmother and Grandfather. I was to be confirmed, and I needed a copy of my birth certificate. That's when Mama finally told me – though she didn't want to – about my real mother, Mary Margaret Griffith. My mother was so ashamed, so guilty, so shunned by her circumstance of being pregnant and unmarried that as soon as she could, she gave her life to Jesus – to God."

"You don't mean…"

"I asked you not to interrupt…please. No she didn't kill herself. That would be a mortal sin – worse than what she had already done. No, she became a nun. She is now in a convent where she devotes her entire life to helping young girls who are in trouble or who might get into trouble. The religious name she selected is Sister Mary Emancipación. I'm sure you know what that means. I never knew the lovely girl she must have been. I have only known the woman whom she became. And I know that it is your fault that she never had a husband, a family, and a happy life. You may ask my forgiveness, and you have it, of course. But I fear that you will never be able to so easily forgive yourself."

"Sister Mary Emancipación! I never would have believed such a thing if you didn't tell me. She was so lively, lovely, and gregarious." André paused and added, "I didn't know they allowed non-virgins to be nuns."

"Of course, they do. They don't allow married women, but they don't hold a woman's past mistakes against her if she truly believes she has a calling, and my mother did feel that calling."

"Do you hate me, Mary Kathryn?"

"No, of course not, but I'm not sure I like you much either. Only time will tell…and please remember to call me Miki. Mary Kathryn sounds like I'm a nun, too."

"There is one thing…uh, Miki. You really need to lose weight. You are too fat. Your mother was so little. How did you get to be so fat?"

"What a thing to say! Go away! Go back to your pathetic studio and think about that for awhile. I am who I am. Take it or leave it."

Miki got up, opened the door, and encouraged André to leave. Then she sat down with the two dogs and cried – and wished she had remembered to purchase ice cream while she was in town. She buzzed Cloud in the kitchen, and Cloud was soon at her cottage door with a carton of Ben & Jerry's New York Super Fudge Chunk and two spoons. They sat down together, shared the ice cream, and talked.

Miki told Cloud what André had said, and Cloud responded, "Don't listen to that crazy old man.

Half the time he doesn't even know who he is or what he's doing. When I first came here, he was drunk as a skunk every single day, and the house was such a mess – stunk like urine and poo! Ick! It took me a long time to clean it up."

"So why did you stay?" Miki asked.

"Well, I needed a job and people around here were kinda wary about hiring me. I have a record, you know – just little stuff – but enough to turn a small town against you."

Miki assured her, "If you're like me, you've screwed up a bunch of things in your life, but all of that is past and it has made you the good person you are today."

The two munched away quietly while the dogs danced around them looking for a bite. Miki told them, "No, you know dogs can't have chocolate! So sit down and behave yourselves." Then she turned back to Cloud, "I understand that André gave you a reading list. How's that going?"

"Okay, I guess. I picked <u>Beloved</u> by Toni Morrison first because I thought it was a love story, but it was really depressing."

"Well, it <u>is</u> a love story – love of mother and child, love of family, but I can see that it probably wasn't what you thought it would be. Whatcha reading now?"

"<u>The Great Gatsby</u> by F. Scott Fitzgerald. I saw the movie. It had Mia Farrow and Robert Redford in it, I think. Anyway, André said it was considered the greatest American novel ever written. So I picked it next. Plus it's short – which is a plus," Cloud said.

"Well, it is a good book. I enjoyed it many years ago, but I would never call it the greatest American novel. I would think that there are several greatest

American novels: <u>Moby Dick</u>, <u>Catcher in the Rye</u>, and certainly <u>The Grapes of Wrath</u>. Sometime let me see your list. I don't suppose he put any Jane Austen on the list – probably too girly for him, but you'd love them – all of them. And you should see if he has a copy of <u>Wuthering Heights</u> and certainly one of <u>Jane Eyre</u>. You'd love those, too. I guess I should go look at his books. I've been wanting to read <u>The Poisonwood Bible</u> by Barbara Kingsolver. If he doesn't have it, maybe we could go to the library some day?"

"Sure. That would be great. Just tell me whenever you want to go to town. I love to do that, and I'd rather drive you in the Escalade than to have you running around in that beat up Volvo of yours"

They both laughed. The ice cream was creamy, chocolatey, and delicious and the conversation was just as scrumptious. They parted so that Cloud could start fixing dinner, and Miki could sneak in a nap.

11. A Person Found

Sitting at the breakfast bar, finishing up the huge breakfast that Cloud prepared every morning, André heard a vehicle come crunching up the gravel drive and onto the smooth parking area and then stop. André got up immediately to see who had come to call. He couldn't see the driver at first, but he saw the old orange Toyota truck and the license plate: *California* TLUCK.

"Robert!" he cried. "It's got to be Robert! Nobody else makes fun of the Chinese as much as Robert does." And he ran outside to greet his long lost friend. Robert got slowly out of the truck and the two one-time buddies hugged each other, patted each other on the back, and patted each other on the butt.

"You old Billy goat," Robert said, "You haven't changed a bit!"

"Horse shit!" André replied, "You are just the same, too…except we are both white haired and wrinkled and probably 'dysfunctional,' too."

"Speak for yourself. I'm still

looking for a rich widder-woman, and I'll make her life a living Shangri-la," Robert bragged.

"I got the last one!" André told him, "But how did you find me?"

"I didn't find you. You found me. That damned private eye of yours tracked me down and half scared me to death! I thought it was one of my ex-wives looking for unpaid alimony or child support. God! I was so relieved when I found out he was your detective and not one of theirs."

"So you've been married and had children?"

"Married four times – two daughters and two sons – somewhere. Don't care where. They are better off without me. You know me. This way they may have a chance for a normal, decent life," Robert answered. "And what have you been up to?"

"Jeepers! Come on in and have a beer. I'll tell you all about it. I'm in the process of trying to round up some of my own kids and bring them here to live – like a family. I have one daughter here already. Remember that adorable little Catholic school girl? Well, this is her daughter."

"Oh, yeah. I think I do remember her. What a doll! Her daughter anything like her?"

"Not a bit. I don't know what happened. I was an Adonis in those days. You gotta admit that, Right? And she was a little doll-baby? But our daughter is pudgy and homely and maybe even a Lezbo!" André admitted.

"Oh, Jeeze, man, I'm sorry. But how many others you got?"

"Well, I have another daughter in San Francisco – daughter of that Miss Chinatown. And I had a son from that rich married woman in Marin County. He died somehow, but his wife and son may come. I just

don't know yet. I've offered all of them a place to live –
all expenses paid. I cannot imagine what there is to
think about. I would think they'd all be here already.
Wouldn't you?"

"Come on, Andy, you gotta admit it's been a
long time. How long ago was that Miss Chinatown
anyway?"

"Oh, God. I don't know – maybe fifty years –
who knows. But the point is that the detective, good old
Bill Simpson, found the kids and I hope they'll all come
here. I got really lonesome and more than a little drunk
after Vivienne died, but now everything's gonna be
okay…specially now that you're here, you old thief!"

Cloud had provided each of the white-haired
men with a beer, and Robert was admiring her young
form. She said, "Get your eyes back in your head, old
man. I'm hired help – not hired meat."

André and Robert both laughed and drank their
beer – trying to think of things to say to each other after
so many years apart. Finally, after another beer (or
two), they began to relive the early years and all the
good times they'd had together plus all the good
women they'd had separately (and sometimes together).

In the middle of this bonhomie, the telephone
rang and Cloud came to tell André that his attorney was
on the phone.

"Oh good. I hope it's good news." He took the
receiver and said, "Yellow?"

"Mr. Zhalovy? This is Connie Evans."

"Yup, have you goddany good news?"

"Mr. Zhalovy, would you like me to call back at
another time? You sound a little sleepy or something."

"'Course not – feel fine. Whasup?"

"You have two more 'yeses.' Mrs. Lerner and
her son, Luke, will be driving up next week, and Mrs.

Aiello wants to fly up and be met at the airport. She'll be there on Thursday next. I thought it would be convenient for me to fly in on the same day, meet her at the airport, and drive down with her from there. That way I will be there to get all the papers signed – if possible. Which reminds me – has Miki signed her papers yet?"

"No, as far as I know, she has not. She's sort of a disagreeable sort of person, isn't she?" André said.

"Oh, I found her to be delightful, but I was only there with her for a very short time. In any case, it surely isn't my place to make judgments of that sort. Will you remember that I will be there with Joy on Thursday next?"

"'Course I will."

"Well, may I speak to Cloud for a moment?"

André handed the receiver back to Cloud who walked with it out to the kitchen. "Sorry about that, Connie, his old friend, Robert turned up today and they've been drinking and reminiscing all afternoon. What do you need?"

"I just want to make sure that you know – that somebody remembers that I will be bringing Joy Aiello up on Thursday next. Her flight gets in at about one o'clock so we'll be there well before dinnertime, I should think And Mrs. Lerner and her son should arrive the same day."

Cloud said enthusiastically, "That's wonderful. I'll get a guest room or two ready. By the way, can I ask you something?"

"Of course."

"Why do you say 'Thursday next' instead of 'next Thursday'?"

Connie laughed and said, "Sorry, I don't mean to sound pretentious or anything like that. I just got in that habit after reading a couple of novels in which a woman named 'Thursday Next' was the main character.[iv] Good books, by the way. You should read them."

"Okay, thanks. Oh, and I should tell you that I'm going to have to put André's friend Robert in one of the cottages so that will leave only the middle cottage free – maybe for the boy? I don't know. I'll have to ask André, when he's sober, if he knows what the boy's interests are so I can decorate accordingly."

"Great. I'll leave it your hands then, Cloud. Good-bye and good luck with those two old men."

"Thanks. I'll need it. Good-bye."

Robert stood up and said, "Man, I gotta pee. Where's the head?"

"Upstairs," André answered, "Out the door and up the stairs."

"You gotta be kidding me! I have to go outdoors and upstairs to pee?! What the Hell?" Robert roared as he went out the door and peed off the porch onto the nearest bare dirt spot in the garden.

"God, Robert, that's disgusting!" Cloud said.

"Well, then tell your stupid boss man here to put in a bathroom downstairs somewhere near where the beer is kept," Robert retorted.

"My wife, Vivienne, didn't want to ruin the Feng Shui of the house," André explained, "so she wanted just the one big room."

"Hell, Andy, you haven't got any Feng Shui anyhow. Sure you got wind and you got water. But your furniture is placed wrong. The chi isn't going to flow anyway. You might as well be smart about this and put in a bathroom down here!"

"So you are a Feng Shui expert now? Are you, Robert?"

"Well, I'm Chinese. I'm closer to the chi than you are, my man. Why don't you just break down and call a contractor while I go help Cloud in the kitchen."

Cloud was cutting up some broccoli and cauliflower to be steamed with carrots and baby new potatoes. She had prepared a beautiful large salmon to be poached, and was stirring a lovely, buttery sauce for it. Plus there was to be strawberry shortcake for dessert.

"Yummy!" Robert said, "It looks like you have things well in hand here."

"Yup," Cloud answered.

"Do you have any extra space in the refrigerator for some of the goodies I brought that require the cold box?" He asked this even as he looked inside the refrigerator and moved things around a little. Then he went out to his truck and brought in a cooler chest packed full of fruit, tofu, Chinese vegetables, frozen wonton, and other things that Cloud couldn't readily identify.

And once that was done he said, "Let me cook tomorrow night – if I can get some fresh seafood in town, or even if not. I'll make you guys some authentic Chinese food. Hope you like that idea."

"You bet," Cloud answered, "I'll even take you to town in the morning and show the best place to shop."

So Robert ferreted around in the cupboards to be sure that they had the bare necessities like salt, white pepper, brown sugar, and arrow root. He also looked through the refrigerator to locate an assortment of veggies to make vegetable stock for soup All of these being present, he was delighted. The next day with Cloud's help, he picked up some jumbo freshwater shrimp, sea scallops, chicken breast/tenders, Shitake mushrooms, green onions, fresh ginger root, and fresh mangos.

That late afternoon and evening found Robert in the kitchen with a nice clean apron. He seemed in his element there and nobody bothered him except as Cloud moved about to get the dishes and silverware to set the dining table for the dinner for five.

Because there was just the cook and not a whole crew in the kitchen, things came to the table one at a time. First was the soup, made with sea weed, flat bean-curd strips, rice stick, and green onion and the previously prepared veggie stock. Then came chunks of canary yellow mangos jostling jade green pea pods and thick strips of sautéed chicken. After that were bok choy hearts under fat juicy mushroom caps in oyster sauce plus al dente long beans tossed with Chinese eggplant, Chinese okra, and tofu. Last of all was mountain of grilled ginger shrimp and scallops topped the sautéed red and yellow peppers, and spring onions all on a bed of Singapore vermicelli.

After setting the last dish down, Robert said, "Oh wait, I forgot the final garnish." He immediately returned to give the seafood a spritz of black sesame oil and bunch of fresh cilantro.

When everything had finally been presented (and half-eaten by André, Miki, Cloud, and Henry ,who had also been invited), Robert was able to join them and enjoy the food as well. He loved to cook, and he loved to eat – but mostly he loved to talk – so everyone else was long finished before Robert was, which was okay because he could then pick at everything and make sure there were no leftovers.

Henry got up and excused himself first, saying only, "Good. Real good. Thanks. Gotta go."

Then Miki helped Cloud clean up the kitchen so she could get going back home before it got too dark to be safe on that twisty road.

12. Thursday Next

The whole household was buzzing and busy when the next Thursday arrived. Miki was helping Cloud get all the rooms and the cottage ready. They'd had to go to town to buy more sheets, pillows, towels, toilet paper, and other supplies. Cloud wanted to buy different colors for each person as she had done for Miki, but was convinced finally that it would be too confusing on laundry days – so they bought all aqua just like Miki's. They bought at Sears, which they felt had a pretty good quality for the money. André wouldn't have cared if they'd bought everything at Neiman Marcus (had there been one in town), but Miki and Cloud were too sensible to pay more than they had to for anything.

Henry spent a lot of time with a contractor from town – one who specialized in remodeling – deciding where and how to put in the new bathroom. The man called himself "The Remodeling Guru" and came highly recommended by other people in town who had used his services.

Robert was in the kitchen making sure there would be plenty to eat when everybody got there. He was doing traditional American this time – a big ham, sweet potatoes with a candied orange sauce, several sorts of vegetables, a spinach salad with prawns, white wine – and fussing and grumbling because no one could tell him for sure what time he should be prepared to serve this feast.

André was in his studio and was not to be disturbed until something really important happened – like a guest arriving, or somebody bleeding or some such emergency.

In the midst of all this, Denzel, who had already found the pool and swam in it regularly also found his way into the house from the pool – just a quick dive under the separating wall – and he stood there as proud as any Lab could  be shaking water all over everything! Denzel was as happy as anything and Cloud and Miki were screaming. That brought André down. When he got there, he laughed and laughed and told everybody that he thought at least a bear had eaten the little, scrawny dog or something interesting like that. It was not the last time that Denzel visited the house in this way.

Just then, a car pulled up out front and everybody (including Denzel) went out to greet the newcomers. Luke popped out of the Subaru Forester first and ran directly to the dog and put his arms around Denzel's wet neck.

"Look, Mom, they have a dog!" Luke exclaimed.

"Yes," Dolly said, "And I hope they have a lady's room. I am so stiff from driving, and I need to go so bad."

Miki said, "Come with me. You can use mine – the others are all upstairs – at least until the contractor finishes putting in a new one."

The two women went off together while Luke assisted Robert, Henry, and André in unloading the car. They put everything on the porch until they could decide what room each person would have. The discussion began as soon as Dolly and Miki came back.

Cloud said, "I have one guest cottage left and two lovely guest rooms on the second floor. Oh, and there is another guest arriving any time now. So you two get to decide first who goes where."

"Oh! Oh! Oh!" Luke cried, "Can I have the guest cottage? Is it in the woods? Can I?"

"Well, Luke, I think it would be better if we were together. Will the cottage hold two people?"

"No, not really. It's actually not that big," Cloud said.

Miki interjected, "Listen, Dolly, he would be right outside the main house, and he would be between Robert and me. I don't think he could get into any trouble from there."

"Yeah, Mom."

"Oh, I don't know. Twelve isn't exactly grown-up, young man. How will I know what you're getting into?" Dolly asked.

"Mom! I never 'get into anything.' You know that."

"Well, okay, but I will be checking on an unannounced regular basis – just like in the army."

"Hooray!" Luke started going through the bags to find his things and then quickly turned to ask André: "Do you have wi-fi?"

"Yes, of course, but be warned, young fella. I also have a LAN[v] and I control it from my studio. I will know if you go to any online spots that you shouldn't be going to, and then your mom will know, too, of course." André said.

"This is a conspiracy," Luke said half-heartedly. "Can I at least invite this great dog into my little house?"

Miki answered, "Of course, if he wants to go. His name is Denzel. He lives with me and my other dog, Punkin, whom you will meet as soon as you go out back. She will bark at you fiercely, but she never bites."

Miki and Dolly went with Luke to the middle guest cottage which he pronounced as being "wicked – blatantly wicked!" And Henry and Robert carried Dolly's things upstairs to the Southwestern most bedroom – the furthest away from André's studio.

Miki had been right about Punkin … she came bounding towards the strangers barking and circling like she were a wolf and getting ready to attack, but Denzel was there, too, and she soon calmed down. She wasn't as cute as she used to be because of being shaved, but she was still a little sweetie pie, and Luke picked her up and carried her along.

Luke was joyful when saw that his cottage was named "Cassiopeia" – a very good sign and a very happy little cottage. He plugged in his laptop right away, looked in the little refrigerator and tried out the bed. "Awesome."

Dolly was mystified by the fact that all the stairs were on the outside of the house, and the explanation about maintaining the Feng Shui didn't influence her a bit. She said, "That's ridiculous! What if there's a fire? Why don't you have that contractor put in an indoor staircase – maybe a spiral staircase – while he's at it?"

Henry went off to suggest this to André and the contractor – who was only too happy to revise his estimate for the work to include a spiral staircase in the house. André said he didn't care – do whatever everybody wants – just get it done.

Later in the afternoon right in the middle of Miki's nap, the dogs set up a fierce barking contest again. Miki assumed that Luke was playing with them or taunting them, but when she got up to check, she discovered that the other guests had arrived.

Connie drove up in her rented Lexus SUV, put the car in park, got out, walked around the car, and opened the passenger door for Joy. Everyone watching knew right away what position Joy held – or thought she held.

Joy greeted them and said, "I am simply exhausted. The damned airlines nowadays. Can you believe what you have to go through at an airport in order to just get on a plane that is only going from San Francisco to Eugene, Oregon? (*She to pronounce it as 'O-rē-gon'*) What? Do they think I am going to blow up Eugene, Oregon? And to have to take your shoes off and parade around in your stockings on that dirty floor!

Well, I'm glad to be here at last. Do I have a room to myself or do I have to camp on the porch?"

Cloud assured her, "We kept the best room for you. It is on the southwestern corner upstairs and will have the best 'chi,' isn't that right, Robert?"

"Absolutely!" Robert agreed, "the very best flow of chi in the whole house."

"Wonderful," Joy replied, "Now would someone carry my bags and show me where to go?"

Henry, Robert, and Luke picked up the great pile of luggage that Joy had arrived with and carried it up to the only remaining guest room. Joy immediately complained about the color of the towels and sheets: "Too much blue is not good," she said, "but I brought my own sheets and towels. Will you have the maid change them for me?"

André was told of this request and went up to pay a visit to Joy. "Hello, Joy. How are you? It's very good of you to come."

"So you are André, is that right?" she asked.

"Yes, I am André as you already know, I'm sure, or you wouldn't be here. I just dropped up for a minute to tell you that we do not have maid service here. I have a girl who comes from town each day and does a little work around the house, but she is not a maid. I'm afraid that the perks of the place do not include maid service. You will have to make your own bed."

"Fine. I've been doing it all my life. I guess I can do it here as well," Joy said.

"Yes, well, I'll talk to you more later."

At dinner that night Joy could see that Cloud had a seat at the table along with everyone else, and that answered her question as nothing else could about what Cloud's status was. So around the table were André,

Miki, Joy, Luke, Dolly, and Cloud. Henry left abruptly after he and the contractor finished with the measurements and plans for the new bathroom and staircase, and Connie had returned to catch her flight to Portland as soon as everyone had seen the legal paperwork that she left for them.

Talk was a little scarce until André asked Luke, "What the hell is that thing plugged into your ear? Are you hard of hearing?"

"Um, no sir, it's my iPod. I'm sorry. I shouldn't be listening to it at the table," Luke said sheepishly.

"Hmmph! What do you listen to?" André wanted to know.

"I was listening to Green Day. He's very cool."

Miki injected, "Oh, _way_ cool. I listen to Green Day, too, sometimes, but I'm much older than you and sometimes I even listen to Billy Joel and the Beatles."

"I listen to the Beatles a lot. I think they are very marvelous," Luke replied.

"Holy cow! I even listen to the Beatles," Robert said, "Anybody listen to Michael Jackson?"

"No. He's a perv."

"What's a perv, Luke?"

"You know, Mom. A pervert, a weirdo. Everybody knows that, Mom," Luke explained.

"Well, he was found not guilty, wasn't he?"

"A fat lot that means," André said, "Look at good old O.J. – fat cat killer."

Miki broke in and said, "Maybe we could talk about something else?"

"Sure," Joy said, "I want to know what we are supposed to do out here in godforsaken rural Oregon now that we don't have jobs to go to?"

André answered, "Whatever you want to do. And, by the way, it's pronounced Oregon (**awr**-i-*guh*n)."

"What? Oh, yes. But I mean **what** am I going to do? I've been thinking about it, and I've worked all my life – even when my babies were little. I can't think what else I know how to do. I've never had any hobbies – just work and get ready for work."

"Well, for one thing you could stop wearing so much make up," Miki said.

"Oh, yes? Well, I can tell you that you would look a lot better if you did wear a little make up," Joy retorted.

"And," Miki pressed on, "you could take off your high-heeled shoes and pantyhose, and let it all hang out like the rest of us."

"I don't 'hang out' even if I try," Joy said.

"Okay. Okay, ladies. That's enough," André said.

But Joy was not satisfied, "If I was as fat as you are, Miki, I'd wear whatever it took to hold it in. Ha. Now, where can I get an ashtray?"

"Nowhere around here" Cloud answered, "This is a strictly non-smoking establishment."

"Great! Just great. I'll go outside then."

"Okay, but be sure to field strip your butts," André said, "Any more wine in that bottle, Robert, or shall I get another."

"I don't think we need another. Let's clean up. I'll wash if somebody wants to dry," Robert said.

"I'll dry," Dolly offered. "I didn't do any of the cooking. You know, we also need to have some sort of a chore list. There's no reason that Cloud and Robert have to do all the cooking, cleaning up, and marketing – or maybe they'd rather do that than dust and vacuum."

André said, "I told Joy that we don't have maid service. And I mean that. Cloud will not clean up your bedrooms and bathrooms. Everyone will be responsible for his or her own area and his or her own laundry – even me, I guess – shit! Excuse my French, but I hadn't thought of that."

Later Robert met up with Joy outside and reminded her, "The Chinese do not show their own thoughts so openly. Put your feelings behind your face. You know your own worth. You don't need to flash it around."

"Robert, anybody can tell that you are a lower class Chinese person. You have the manners and wit of a coolie. So you don't need to offer me any advice on how to live my life."

"Oh, yes?" Robert said, "Well, may this lowly peasant at least advise you to quit smoking? It's ruining your health and making your skin look leathery, my dear."

13. What People Say

A couple of days later, the women decided to go on a shopping trip to town. Cloud drove, leaving Robert at home to supervise the remodeling, Luke to watch the dogs, Henry to weed the gardens, and André to do whatever it was that André did. The four ladies set off in high good spirits – until Joy wanted to light up a cigarette at which everyone else protested and pretended to cough to death. Joy decided she could wait.

Cloud drove to the main shopping center in town and let Miki, Joy, and Dolly out to do whatever they wanted to do. Cloud had a shopping list for groceries and supplies which had been contributed to by everyone other than André and Henry, and the other ladies had things they wanted to purchase as well. André had given the three women plus Luke each a MasterCard® of their own so that they could shop. The bills would all come to him, and he would pay them. Luke wanted to use his to shop online, but the women wanted to actually go to the stores and touch the things they bought.

"I'm going to the supermarket," Cloud announced, "and I'll be back in about an hour or so. If you can, meet me near the mall entrance at Sears, and we can plan to go to lunch somewhere nice."

Miki went off by herself to the camera store. There were so many beautiful things to take pictures of – including, of course, Punkin and Denzel. Thus, she had decided to take up photography in a more serious way. She had a camera, of course, but it wasn't digital. And she wanted to be able to load the pictures directly into her computer where she could organize them and remove red-eye and such. She looked at the various cameras, and finally got a salesperson to help her decide what she needed, being an amateur and all. After considering the various qualifications of each model and the prices, she selected a Canon Power Shot A570IS digital with 4x optical zoom and 7.1 mega pixels for high-resolution shots. She also bought an extra memory card, extra batteries, a nice carrying case, an HP printer, and the photo paper she would need. She was very excited about getting started with this new pasttime.

Dolly didn't really need much. She went to Rite-Aid and bought a couple of night lights, some 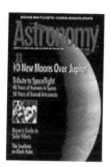 extra batteries for Luke, and the *Astronomy* magazine that Luke wanted. Next, she went to Sears where she got some new underwear for herself and for Luke. She looked at the hiking boots, but decided that the ones they had could make it through another season. She also bought herself a bathrobe – she'd never had one – never found it necessary until now to cover her pj's if she got up before getting fully dressed. She wondered if she should get one for Luke, too, and then decided against it.

Joy had gone directly to Macy's, which she considered the only store in the center that was "decent." She'd said, "What a shame that you don't have a Nordstrom's here, but Macy's will do in a pinch."

After trying on many pairs of flat-heeled shoes, she finally bought three pairs of alligator loafers: one black, one navy, and one red. She also picked up several pairs of knee-high sheer stockings, three pairs of twill trousers (in different colors), three knit tops, three silk blouses, four new bras (of different colors), six new hip-hugger panties, a blue windbreaker, and a bottle of Tresemmé®. Then she went on to the jewelry department and picked out some earrings and bracelets to go with her new outfits. In the "home" department, she bought a French tea press and clock radio/CD player. When she was finished she had more bags than she could comfortably carry – so she asked one of the salespersons to carry everything over to where she was to meet her friends.

Everyone was there waiting. Cloud asked, "Do you have a watch, Joy? We've been waiting for almost an hour here."

Joy responded, "Well, you could have come down to Macy's. I wouldn't have shopped anywhere else. In fact, you could have helped carry all these bags."

"Oh holy cow!" Cloud said, "I hope we can fit that all in along with all the groceries and supplies that we all needed or wanted."

Miki and Dolly helped Cloud load the back of the Escalade and then asked, "Where shall we go to lunch?"

"There's an Applebee's very close by," Cloud told them, "or we can go to the Sizzler or Red Robin. What would everyone like to do?"

"I vote for Applebee's," Miki said.

"I second that," Dolly quickly added.

"Well," Joy said, "I guess that will be okay."

The four had a good lunch. Miki had riblets with French fries. Dolly had a steak sandwich also with fries. Cloud had a spicy chicken salad. And Joy – after much muttering – ordered onion soup served in a bread bowl. They all (except Cloud) had strawberry Daiquiris. Cloud was driving, and so she had a strawberry/banana smoothie. The food was good. The drinks were yummy. And the conversation was patchy at best.

None of them knew what to talk about. No one knew what to say. They were family, and yet they were not. What a contrast between them! A very thin Chinese banker, a pudgy Catholic teacher, a robust Jewish forester, and a pierced kid from town. They really didn't consider this contrast, and they didn't notice the people around them looking and whispering.

Miki wanted to know why Joy bought only at Macy's, and Joy said, "I deserve good things. I have good Karma."

Joy wanted to know how Dolly got that name, and Dolly said, "My real name is Deirdre, but I've always been called Dolly – except by my professors and my in-laws."

Dolly wondered whether Miki wanted to get in shape because she (Dolly) could help her with that, and Miki said, "Golly, anybody would think that I was three hundred pounds the way everyone picks at me, but I'm actually very healthy and very happy. My cholesterol is low, my blood pressure is good, and my attitude about the whole thing was fine until you and André said something about it."

Dolly immediately apologized, "I shouldn't butt into your business anyway. I just want to get to know you and know what you like and don't like and stuff like that."

Cloud offered, "Well, she likes chocolate and so do I!"

All four women agreed on that and congratulated Cloud when she told them that she'd bought several cartons of ice cream that they could get into whenever they wanted to. After lunch, the women went back to André's place – their place.

But the people in town were soon spreading rumors: André was creating a commune out there on Vivienne's property, they said. It's a lesbian commune, someone else said. Hell, it's a Chinese-communist commune other people said. They'd seen that Chink the other day and today that Chinese woman. And they all looked Lezbo, didn't they? All except one had very short dyke hair, didn't they? And the only one with long hair dressed like a logger or something. Yup, it must be true – a Lesbian/Communist cult. Yeah, but someone else had heard that one them was Jewish. Of course, so is that old man – they knew that for sure.

These rumors spread and grew to the point where it was assumed to be true, and that night when Cloud went home, her aunt asked her, "What the Hell is going on out there where you work for that dirty old man?"

Innocently, Cloud asked, "Whatcha mean?"

"Oh, it's all over town that he's setting up a commune or a cult or something like that out there. Didn't we have enough trouble right here in Oregon with cults already. Remember the Rashneeshees?"

Cloud replied, "Oh, Aunt Gerry, this is nothing like that. This is just one old man trying to get to know his family."

Aunt Gerry retorted, "His family? I heard that there was a Chinaman and a Chinese woman and that all of the females are lesbians. Is that so?"

"God! I don't know. I don't think so. They all seem perfectly normal to me," Cloud said.

"Yeah, well what do you know? You're just a kid, and you look and dress funny anyway."

"Well, don't spread the rumor around because I don't think it's true, and it could really hurt those people. They are nice – mostly. And besides that, it's a good job – better than any other I could get around here."

"I know what!" said Aunt Gerry just as if Cloud weren't there, "I'll ask Henry. He may be a little slow, but he'll know. Next time he comes in for pie and coffee, I'll ask him."

And he did come in later that night for his usual cherry pie and coffee. "You want that heated and with ice cream?" Gerry asked.

"Yup."

When she served Henry's pie, Gerry asked him, "Hey, Henry, what's going on out at Vivienne's place?"

"Well, we're putting in a new bathroom and a staircase that goes up in a circle like a corkscrew," Henry said with his mouth full of pie and ice cream. "Ooh, cold. Wow! That's cold ice cream."

"Henry, that's not what I meant – I mean what's going on with all the people. Folks around here say that André is starting a commune for Lezbos and Commies. Is that right?" Gerry pushed him further.

"Lezbos and Commies! Really? I didn't know that. I just thought it was André's friends. I don't want to work there if it's for Lezbos and Commies!" Henry cried.

"Now, Henry, we don't know for sure – yet. Do we? We need you to find out and tell us what's going on. Can you do that?" Gerry asked.

"Sure, I guess so." He paused, "How do I do that? And what's a Lezbo anyway?"

Gerry instructed him, "Never mind, Henry, just watch and listen and then let me know what you see and hear. In fact, Henry, I'll give you free pie each time you bring me some info from out there."

Henry perked up, "With ice cream?"

"Sure – maybe even extra ice cream," Gerry promised. "Just let me know what you find out before you tell other folks. Okay?"

"Okay. Sure. I guess that's okay," Henry said as he finished his pie and coffee.

No one back at André's house had any idea this was going on. Cloud had an idea of the rumors, of course, but she didn't tell the others. And after dinner that night, the women decided that they would have an informal meeting tomorrow to talk and make suggestions and lists for how they wanted to make this "family" thing work. They also agreed that they would all bring their legal papers with them, and decide whether to sign them.

Before going to bed, Dolly tapped at her son's cottage door, "Luke, are you in there? Are you awake?"

The door flew open, and a very excited Luke said, "Mom! You gotta see what I found online. Holy cow! This is so very **wicked**! I went to Astronomics.com and clicked on Celestron because I know those are the **best**. I found two that I really, really like. And now I can't decide which one I want."

Dolly hugged him and asked, "Why don't you show them to me?"

So back Luke went to the Astronomics site and showed his mother first the Celestron 4.7" Omni XLT 120 equatorial refractor with Starbright XLT optical multicoatings. "See," he said, "this one is great. It has a 'dew shield' and a 'rack and pinion focuser' with a 'finderscope' and all the software so I can chart the skies. And it costs $599.00 plus $50.00 for shipping."

"Okay," Dolly said, "let's see the other one."

Luke then went to the next site and said, "Okay, now this one is the Celestron 5" Omni XLT 127 equatorial Schmidt-Cassegrain with Starbright XLT optical multicoatings. This is a refractor telescope – much more advanced than the other, and it's only $699.00 with the $50.00 for shipping."

"And you can't decide. Is that right?"

"Well, I guess I could decide. The first one is really the best one for a beginner like me, I suppose. I just thought the other one was really, really spectacular."

"I agree with you. The first one is the best for you, and that's the one I think you should start with. You can go on to something bigger and better after you learn more about what you're doing. Is that acceptable?"

Luke said, "That's terrific! I'll order it right now. What's the address here?"

"Good grief. I don't know. Let me find out."

So Dolly buzzed André in the main house and asked him, "What's the address here? Luke wants to have something shipped here."

André answered, "I just have everything shipped to me at the post office which is on Kane Street downtown. Have him put in care of André Zhalovy, and it will get here just fine. Oh, and tell him to have it shipped Fed-Ex, they are the ones who will leave it there. UPS always wants me to come to town and sign for things."

14. Meeting & Agreeing

Cloud organized a nice place for the "family" meeting the very next day. She set up a picnic table and several chairs in the shade of the huge big leaf maple tree which was far enough away from the house so that they wouldn't be overheard but close enough for potty-runs and such. She also provided iced-tea and a plateful of homemade chocolate chip cookies.

Miki was the first one to arrive – with a yellow pad and two No.2 pencils for taking notes. However, Dolly brought a laptop, so the yellow pad was sort of redundant. Luke was there, also. And last to show up was Joy.

Joy asked, "Is Cloud supposed to be part of this meeting? I mean, she's not part of the family."

"Of course, she should be here," Miki said. "She usually has really good ideas – she's wise for her age – and a lot of the stuff we're going to discuss definitely affects her directly."

Joy retorted, "I suppose all the piercings and tattoos are a sign of her 'wisdom'?"

"I only have one tiny tattoo, and that's in a place where you'll never, ever see it!" Cloud retorted.

Dolly said, "Okay, let's not judge people here. Let's talk about what we came here for, and that is: how are we going to make this work? Do we want to make this work? Are we all going to sign the papers that Connie gave us?"

"So I'll ask again, what do women do with their time when they have worked all their lives and have no hobbies and no little grandchildren under foot and so on?" Joy questioned.

Cloud returned with, "What do you think of when you look around this place? I know for me it's easy – it means the best job I've ever had … and a free education being around all of you plus André's huge book collection. But it will also mean going completely nuts if someone doesn't help me sometimes."

Miki said, "Good point, Cloud. Well, when I look around, I see freedom. No more alarm clocks. No more trying to pound Algebra into heads that still don't know their multiplication tables. And my little cottage is my sanctuary. And it is joyful for my Denzel and Punkin."

Luke added, "Yeah, freedom…and really dark skies at night so I can see the stars clearly when my telescope gets here…and Miki's dogs, of course."

"Freedom is such a good answer," Dolly said, "Yes, and I see the forest. It looks like it hasn't been taken care of – maybe <u>ever</u>. I see opportunity. How about you, Joy?"

Joy lit a cigarette and waved her hand through the smoke as if brushing gnats away. "Oh, I don't know," she said, "I guess I see freedom, too, but to do what, I don't know. I also see the great house and the inheritance. Is everybody going to sign the papers that Connie gave us?"

"Yes, I know I will," Miki said, "I don't want to go back to California. This is just a great place, and I know I'm going to enjoy my new camera. I haven't had much of a chance to try it out yet, but I'm really looking forward to it. I'm going to need some better shoes though. I took a look at the trail up into the forest and concluded that even walking shoes won't do the trick."

"Yeah, that's right, Miki," Dolly said, "I will wear my calked boots when I go in there. It's going to be impossible to walk through there otherwise.

"And you know what I think? I think each of us should find what gives us joy and go with it. As you know, Luke has ordered a telescope and will be getting more and more into astronomy. But let's talk for a minute about what we can all do to help Cloud around the house."

"Okay, what about it? What can we do?" Miki asked.

"Well, to start with, I think everyone should do their own laundry like André suggested. It's not like it's any real trick with the automatic washer and dryer," Cloud said.

"Yeah, I think we can all agree to that."

Joy asked, "Is there a place in town that does fine and delicate things?"

"Sure," Cloud answered, "the dry cleaners also handles special laundry. I can take your stuff to town whenever you need me to."

Dolly said, "Okay, now I don't think that Cloud should have to cook and clean up every night. I think we should take turns with that."

"I don't know how to cook," Miki said, "I've always had roommates who liked to cook. I don't suppose they deliver pizza clear out here, do they?"

"No, they don't. But I can teach you a few tricks in the kitchen – or Robert could," Cloud suggested.

"Oh, heaven save me from Robert! Did you ever hear anybody talk as much and say as little as he does?"

"You're right. He is so funny."

"So let me get this down," Dolly said, "Everyone will clean their own space plus their bathroom – including Luke. And everyone will do their own laundry, and we will take turns cooking and cleaning up. Do we want to make a schedule? I can do that right now."

"Sure – let's make this official and post it on the refrigerator. I'll be partners with Cloud. She can teach me what to do, and when she cooks, I'll clean up. When I cook, she cleans up. Okay?" Miki said.

"Great, and I'll be partners with Luke," Dolly said. "When I cook, he'll clean up. And when he cooks, well he & I will cook and clean up together."

"Oh thanks a bunch!" Joy cried, "That leaves me with Robert. Well, at least I know a few ways to get that old man to shut up ... some old 'Confucius Say' items that I can throw out at him."

Everyone laughed together. "See we are becoming more like a family all the time."

Just then Henry came over and wanted to know if he could join the party. "I want to be part of the family, too," he said.

"Of course, Henry, you are part of the family," Cloud said, "but you have enough work to do already with all the gardening and repairs and keeping the pool clean."

"Yup," Henry said, "'Nuff to do. That's for sure. But can I have dinner and help with that, too?"

"Well, I don't know," Cloud said, "I'll ask André if it's okay with him. I know that I'm cooking tonight – and you're more than welcome tonight."

"Okay, dinner tonight," Henry said "An' you wanna know what Gerry said? Gerry said that this is a commune or a cult or something and that you all are communists. Is that right? Are you really communists?"

"No, Henry, we're not communists. We're just family – and now you're part of the family," Miki said.

"Well, okay," Henry said happily and went back to his work pulling weeds out of the flower gardens.

"I hope he doesn't try to take advantage of that," Joy said, "I don't think there's room for him to move in with the rest of us. Anyway, we still haven't decided what women do when they have nothing to do. You know what I mean? So Miki will take pictures, and Luke will look at the stars, and Dolly will tramp around in the woods. How much time will that take? What about the rest of the time? And what will I do? I've never had a hobby – never."

"Do you play games? Could we play cards or something?" Miki asked.

"No, I've never learned to play anything – well, anything except the piano. I guess I could get back into that. André does have a beautiful piano," Joy said.

Dolly offered, "You have a computer, don't you? Why don't you write a book? I bet you have had some really interesting experiences working in a bank in San Francisco all these years, and especially with your Chinese heritage."

"I could do that," Joy said. "Yes, I could. I'd be able to write a very good book. I've done so much writing in my career – instruction booklets, procedure manuals, and so forth. It can't be too much different writing a book."

"Okay," Dolly said, "I have the schedule. Let's see if it appears acceptable to everyone: Sunday – Cloud cooks, Miki cleans up; Monday – Dolly cooks, Luke cleans up; Tuesday – Joy cooks; Robert cleans up; Wednesday Miki cooks, Cloud cleans up; Thursday Luke cooks and Dolly cleans up; Friday Robert cooks and Joy cleans up. That just leaves Saturday – what do we do with Saturday?"

"Wait a minute, let's shove all those days one day ahead and leave Sunday open, because I don't work on Sunday," Cloud said. "You can all go out to eat on Sunday – or have PB&J's. By the way, I cook breakfast for André every day except Sunday, but I don't cook for the whole family. Okay? And please put your rinsed dishes all the way into the dishwasher instead of on the counter."

"Right. Yes. Okay. I forgot about Sundays. Let's start this on Monday with Cloud cooking and Miki cleaning up. Do we need a laundry schedule? Or can we just sort of work around each other?" Dolly queried.

"Oh for goodness sake, we're all grown-ups! Well, most of us are. Let's see if we can just get along."

Cloud added, "I am a little concerned about what Henry said. You know, about being a commune or a cult. We don't want those types of rumors getting started in town. For heaven's sake, the town's people are, in general, very nice, but there is also the Redneck crowd and a certain number of skinheads – Aryan Nation types. I don't want any of us to have any trouble. I'll talk to my Aunt Gerry tonight and try to put a stop to this sort of talk."

"Great. Now, when shall we go to town and have our signatures on these agreements witnessed and copied for us and for Connie?"

Cloud said, "The bank is closed tomorrow, and I'm off on Sunday. You wanna go right now?"

So all of them got their identification and their legal papers and went off to the bank where the bank manager watched them sign, witnessed each signature, notarized each (just in case it might be needed), and produced copies. She mailed the originals to Connie in Portland and gave copies to the women along with those for André.

"Okay, we're in for it now!"

15. A Sticky Situation

Dolly laced up her calked boots (the boots that foresters wear with the spikes on the bottom for traction) and rolled her knee socks down over the top of each boot. She wanted to get out into the woods and have a look around. Luke insisted on going along. He had hiking boots but no calked boots so he'd have to be extra careful … but he knew that. He'd been in the woods before … actually since before he could walk, riding around in his mother's backpack. He asked Miki if Denzel could come, too, and she okayed that. It was obvious that Punkin couldn't come. She just was <u>not</u> a woodsy type of dog.

Dolly had put through a call to the Land Conservation and Development Commission (LCDC) to find out how Oregon state laws might affect the forest land. She hadn't had a call back yet, but she'd gone to the Website at www.oregon.gov/LCD/forlandprot.shtml and quickly read through the items that were covered there. An owner of private forest land needed permits for everything that was done on the land plus consideration of:

- Road access design
- Fuel-free buffers
- Chimney spark arresters
- Public or contracted fire protection
- Water availability
- Maximum grade for building site

She would have to go to the State Forestry Department in town down by the airport and get a permit to use mechanical tools in the woods: chain saws, Cats, yarders, whatever. And she'd need a "salvage" permit in order to be able to remove the deadfall and trees in the way of the road.[vi] Dolly hoped that some of these other requirements wouldn't apply to what she wanted to do since André had long had a dwelling on the site. But she would have to talk to him about what sort of fire protection he had or contracted for. The proximity of the river would take care of the water requirement.

As she tramped up into the woods, she had to cut through some of the heavy undergrowth with a Sandvik to make a path. "Holy cow," she said to Luke, "some of these rhododendrons are ten feet tall. And look at all the dead fall. This is prime fire country unless this is cleaned out."

"Yeah, I know," Luke responded, "And the trees are all different sizes…a fire would go up them just like climbing a step ladder."

"Yup. This needs a lot of work – cleaning out, thinning, cutting, and spraying – the works. I guess I'd better get together with André and find out how much of this he wants me to do and how much we should contract out. But it definitely needs attention."

"God! It's beautiful though, isn't it, Mom?"

"Oh, yes, it's like a cathedral – it lifts your eyes up and up towards the high pinnacles at the tops of the trees. No wonder city folks don't want us to cut any of these trees. It's just that they don't understand that a forest that is managed properly is a much healthier forest," Dolly said.

Meanwhile, Denzel was running around through the trees and the undergrowth and having the wonderful time that only a dog can have because every day is a new adventure – a new smell – a new sight. Luke called to him from time to time, and Denzel would come crashing though to the path that Dolly was making. This time they heard Denzel before they saw him. He howled in pain and came running to Luke with a snout full of porcupine quills. He howled and howled as if to say, "Ow! Ow!"

Dolly said, "Let's head back. We need to get this poor dog to the Vet right away. Porcupine quills not only hurt, but they can be very dangerous. In the future, he may steer clear of porcupines, but we'd better put together a 'quill kit' just in case."

They hurried back through the forest with Luke leading the way, and found Miki. Cloud heard the fuss that Miki just naturally made when she saw her beautiful Denzel. Cloud drove Miki, Luke, and Denzel to the "best Vet in town" – Dr. Wayne.

The Umpqua River Veterinary Hospital was just on the outskirts of town, and the doctor was in. The receptionist took Denzel's

information from Miki while Luke took Denzel back to see the doctor. While they waited, they watched Dr. Wayne check a small dog that looked a lot like Punkin. She was getting older and just needed to be looked over to make sure she was in good shape, and the doctor suggested only that she needed more exercise and a less table scraps.

When he got to Denzel, Dr. Wayne was only too familiar with this type of situation. He sprayed Denzel's muzzle with an anesthetic and then after a short wait, during which Miki joined them, he asked Luke to hold the dog while he snipped each quill with scissors to let some of the air around the quill escape. Then he pulled the quills one by one with needle-nose pliers. He held the flesh downward while he pulled each, and the poor dog flinched at each extraction. He then checked the dog carefully to make sure there were no hidden quills in the ears, mouth, or between the pads on the feet.

The doctor said, "It's good that you brought this fella in right away. A quill starts working it's way into the flesh just as soon as it is injected and that can be very dangerous."

"Oh, thank you, doctor," Miki said.

"In the future, if you need to do this yourself, soak the area with vinegar to soften up the quills and then snip them off and pull them out," the Vet advised.[vii]

"Okay," Miki said, "but that would hurt him, wouldn't it?"

"Well, yes, there would be considerably more pain, but it would also be quicker if it happens in the middle of the night or some such thing. I'll send home some spray-on anesthetic that should help a lot. However, you can call me anytime, I'm usually around most of the time. I don't like to leave the animals here alone."

Miki paid the Vet's bill and took one of his business cards so that she'd have his number handy whenever she needed it. When they were back in the car, Miki asked Cloud, "Is Dr. Wayne married?"

"Uh, no, I don't think so, Miki. Why? You interested?" Cloud answered.

"Well, maybe. He seems near my age and not at all bad looking," Miki said and giggled girlishly.

When they got home, Dolly wanted to pay for the Veterinarian – because she said it was her fault, "I just feel so bad about this. We should have kept better track of Denzel."

Miki reminded her, "First of all, it was not your fault. Dogs are dogs. And besides that, I used the MasterCard that André gave me. I just hope my boy doesn't get into it with a porcupine again – or any other wild animals out there in the woods. Are there other animals out there? What do you think?"

Dolly said, "Of course. There are lots of deer tracks around the yard every morning. They probably come during the night to snack on Henry's flowers. And this morning I saw scat from skunks, porcupines, and bear. I just hope there aren't any cougar out here. You know the state has laws about hunting bears and cougars – so now there are more than ever, and they're getting closer and closer to civilization looking for food."

"Holy cow! Dolly, maybe you should have a gun when you go into the woods!" Miki exclaimed.

"I do. Don't worry. I do. I take a 357 magnum with me when I go out. I just don't tell everyone about it," Dolly said, "I wouldn't let Luke go with me without taking a gun to protect him. I'm personally so conceited that I think I can climb a tree faster than a bear, but I'm not dumb enough to think I could get away from a cougar."

André came walking out of the house as they drove up at home, and patted Denzel, "Poor fellow. I'm sorry about those neighbors there in the woods, but their family was here before mine. So, Dolly, can I talk to you and Luke for awhile? I'd like to get to know you a bit better."

Dolly said, "You can talk to me, André, but I think Luke has other things he'd like to do, don't you Luke? Yes, you do – go on now." Luke went off to his cottage, and Dolly asked André if they could go up to her room so they could talk privately. They walked up the stairs and made themselves comfortable in her room.

"So tell me about yourself, Dolly."

"What do you want to know, André? Do you really want to know about me or do you want to know about your son, Max?"

"I guess I want to know everything – you and Luke and Max and his mother. It's been a lot of years since I saw Dorothy. Is she still married to that old Jew?"

"Yes, Dorothy and Jacob are still together and still living in Marin County."

"Are you a Jew, Dolly?" André asked.

"Would it make a difference if I were?" she retorted.

"No, of course, not – just curious."

"Well, I'm not. I was a Presbyterian, but Luke's father was Jewish and I know that Dorothy and Jacob, his grandparents would want Luke to remain a Jew also. He should have his Bar Mitzvah on his 13th birthday in November, but he's never been educated in the Jewish traditions and laws. I'm not sure yet what I'll do about that, but I hope you will be proud of him whatever happens."

"Of course. Of course. But what about Max? What happened to Max?"

Dolly sighed deeply and said, "Maxwell was my soul mate, my one and only love. We met in college. We married right after graduation and were together almost every day until he died. He had a back injury from a bad jump when fighting a fire. He was a smoke jumper, you see, because he could augment our income that way while I worked at a desk and took care of the baby. Well, the back injury led to pain meds. The pain meds led to drinking and stronger pain meds. And all that led to drinking and Meth – and eventually an overdose."

"Oh my God! That's dreadful! Was there nothing you or Dorothy could do to help him?"

"We tried, André. We really tried."

"Well, evidently you didn't try hard enough. My only son and you let this happen to him!"

"Go to Hell, André! Where were you? Where you when Dorothy gave birth to a baby that Jacob knew damned well wasn't his? Where were you when Max was growing up and wondering why he didn't look like his siblings? Where were you when Max worked his way through college fighting wildfires? Where were you when he fell? Where were you – you damned stupid old man!"

"God! I'm sorry," André said as he held up both hands defensively.

"No. No, you're not. You're not sorry at all. I don't believe that you have ever thought of anyone but yourself in your whole life! Why are there no pictures of your wife in the house? Do you remember her? Do you ever think of her? Or is two years too long to try to remember anyone?"

"You are a prickly little thing, my dear. And what about Luke. Does he blame me, too? Does he hate me, too?" André asked.

"None of us hate you, André. We just don't like you. Can you blame us? And Luke doesn't know what to think. You are just an extra person in his life."

"Okay. I get it. By the way, I hear that you want to manage my forest land – well, go right ahead. I give you my permission to manage the forest land. Contract out what you need to in order to have it done right. Meanwhile, I'll try to think about you and the others once in awhile."

16. Joy's Mask

> Man only likes to count his
> troubles, but he does not count
> his joys.
> ~ Fyodor Dostoyevsky

Joy woke up the next morning with a migraine headache. She hadn't had one in a long time. In fact, she had thought that they were from the stress of her job, which was certainly no longer present. But she pulled herself up out of an profound dream in which she had been fighting with the President of her bank. *He wouldn't give her a letter of recommendation in spite of the fact that she had nothing but glowing reviews in her personnel file. She argued that he could not ethically deny what she had accomplished with her efforts with the shaping of his retail operations. He argued that she had "no right" to know what was in her personnel file, and therefore how could she possibly know what he thought of the work she had done? She contended in return that he had no power to take the years and the accomplishments away from her, and if he did, well, she would – she would tell his wife about all of his affairs. He was irate that she would threaten him ...he yelled at her!*

Thus, when Joy did wake up, she was fuming mad and exhausted from arguing with her imaginary boss. She pulled on the dressing gown that she kept across the bottom of her bed and wandered into the bathroom to get a Tylenol with Codeine that the doctor had prescribed for her headaches. Then she got back into bed and covered her eyes with her sleep mask.

She did not go back to sleep. She just lay there waiting for the pain pill to take effect and soften the pain and take away the shimmering half moon that blocked her vision. She thought about where she was and what she was doing and what she might do in the future. The house was nice. She liked it. She had to admit that, and she liked her room a lot. It was large and light with plenty of room for all of her things – she had put out framed photographs of family and friends on the shelves that had been provided for something – whatever she wanted, she supposed. She also got out her original Chinese silk embroideries. She'd have to have Henry hang those for her. She didn't want to ask André or Robert to do that. She didn't like them. Well, she didn't actually like any of them. They gave her the creeps!

She also had her Buddha sitting on the desk next to her laptop – this one was the reclining Buddha – her favorite. She had others with her but she hadn't placed them yet. She wanted to be sure that they were in the most favorable places. She was not, in fact, a Buddhist, but she was closer to that than anything else, and it helped with the persona she had established for herself.

So she smiled behind her mask, she was actually quite comfortable here, and – yes, happy. But she didn't want any of the others to know. She didn't want any of them to know anything about her. She had erected her protective wall and didn't want any cracks in it. She thought Miki was dumpy-looking and not the sharpest knife in the drawer – but so very kind and so appealing.

It was impossible not to like Miki. Dolly was sort of a mystery, but she was sharp as a tack and very fit – as was her son. In fact, Luke was a great kid. She sort of liked both of them, too. And in spite of herself, she liked Cloud. She felt like Cloud could be a daughter figure – someone she could mold and shape to be a decent lady. She wondered how Cloud was doing on her reading. Reading is a great thing…no one is wiser than those who read.

Then there was a light tap-tapping at the door, and Cloud called, "Joy, are you all right? Are you in there?"

"Come on in, Cloud," Joy said.

"Oh, are you ill? Do you need something?" Cloud asked as she came into the room.

"It's one of my migraines. Do you have any chamomile or chrysanthemum tea? These are Chinese teas that are good for headache. Perhaps Robert would have some – or feverfew if he has it."

"I'll see what I can find. Do you want any breakfast?" Cloud inquired quietly.

"Oh, God, no! I cannot eat anything when my head hurts like this. No. Just tea."

So Cloud went away in search of Robert to see if he had any Chinese tea or "feverfew" whatever that was.

"No feverfew," Robert told her when she found him still eating breakfast, "but I do have chrysanthemum tea which is properly called Xia Sang Ju, but she should know that it is good for colds and fever – not headaches. I think she is just pulling your chain. She just wants attention. I'll take her some ordinary tea with honey in it. I bet she won't know the difference."

"Okay," Cloud agreed, "but she really did seem to be sick – with her eyes covered against the light."

Robert made a special small pot of tea and put it on a tray along with the china cup and saucer and silver spoon. He was going up the stairs to deliver the tea when he was waylaid by André, who wanted to talk to Joy and would take the tea to her.

André tapped on the door and then walked right in. He set the tea tray on the table next to the bed and pulled a chair up beside her as well. He sat, and said, "Good morning, Joy. I've brought the special tea that Robert concocted for you. I'll pour, shall I?"

"I guess so. What are you doing in here? I asked Cloud to bring me tea – not to have it delivered by you of all people. My headache is bad enough already."

André spoke quietly, "Well, do try to sit up a little and have a sip of tea. It will make you feel stronger, and then maybe you can talk to me for a bit. I'd really like to get to know you a little better. I've talked to the others, and now I'd like you to tell me about yourself."

Joy sat up as André piled a bunch of her pillows behind her. She sipped the tea, and said, "Yes, this is good chrysanthemum tea. Robert would know."

"I'll tell him you're pleased," André said. "But do I detect the slight odor of cigarette smoke? Have you been smoking in my house, Joy?"

"Just one – to help the headache – and I practically fell out of the window trying to get the smoke to go outside. So, anyway, what do you want to know about me that your lawyer and private detective didn't already tell you?"

"Just everything. I know you were a successful career woman and that you have been married more than once and have two successful children, but I don't know anything about <u>you</u> – about who you are and what you like. I don't know anything about your childhood or your schooling. I remember your mother very well. She was beautiful and delicate. Do you have any pictures of her?"

"My mother is a 'ghost' that I am forbidden to talk about. And what do you care anyway? I am fifty-one years old, and you have never attempted to contact me in all those years. The accident of my birth should mean nothing to you. You contributed at least one fast swimming sperm, and I am the result. I am not your daughter, Mr. Zhalovy, though I have signed your agreement and will gladly live in your house and take your money."

"Why is your mother a 'ghost' to you? Why are you forbidden to talk about her?" André asked.

"People who shame their families…people who cause their family to lose face … are ghosts and are not spoken of," Joy answered.

"Just because she got pregnant? Is that what happened? Did her family shun her because of that?"

Joy sighed profoundly and said, "Okay, pretend for a moment that I am speaking of another – a pretend person – a ficticious Chinese girl who is beautiful and graceful and full of virtue. Pretend for a moment that this person of whom I speak is so beautiful that she is crowned Miss Chinatown San Francisco, and her family is proud and has her picture in the window of their storefront. They brag about her to everyone. Then supposing this young unwed beauty queen becomes suddenly pregnant – her stomach pushing out the front of her beautiful gowns. The people laugh at her and point and laugh at the family and point at the picture in the storefront. And the girl gives birth to a healthy baby girl, and then goes out midway on the Golden Gate

Bridge and jumps into the Bay and is killed, of course. Would this family not lose face? Would this person not be a 'ghost' forever?"

"Oh my God," André said. "I am so sorry. I didn't know. I didn't even guess. How could I conceivably have known?"

"Yes," Joy said between her teeth, "how could you conceivably have known?"

"So were you adopted out or did you grow up with your grandparents?"

Joy answered quietly, "I grew up with an aunt and uncle who were very good to me in spite of my low birth. They gave me everything they gave their own children, and they helped me get my degree from the University of San Francisco. I owe them much and I revere them as my true parents."

"You seem to have a lot of wisdom, Joy. Perhaps someday you can forgive me, and we can be friends."

"Mahatma Gandhi has said, 'The weak can never forgive. Forgiveness is the attribute of the strong.' And, whereas I do forgive you, I doubt that I will ever like you, André. Therefore, I doubt that we can ever be friends. But perhaps if you put your mind to it, you could learn to like me. You might also think about this quote from Confucius: 'To put the world in order, we must first put the nation in order; to put the nation in order, we must put the family in order; to put the family in order, we must cultivate our personal life; and to cultivate our personal life, we must first set our hearts right.'"

"Quotations …quotations. Have you no original thoughts?" André retorted.

"Yes, I do. Let's see…Joy says, 'Man who come into lady's room uninvited, soon find himself in deep shit.' So now get out of my room!"

17. What's Up At Night?

The telescope finally arrived. It was one of the most exciting days of Luke's life. A phone call had come from town that there was a package waiting, and he could not wait a minute for someone to take him to town. Cloud wasn't doing much anyway, but he had to wait until she got to the end of a chapter in the book she was reading. She told him, "I don't like to leave things in the middle 'cause then I forget what's happening and have to go back and read part of it again."

But they finally got the package and got it home. Luke recruited Henry, Robert, and André to come out and help him put it together, but none of them were really very useful. Robert read the instructions so slowly that it would be a week before the thing was up and ready. And André just sat and supervised while Henry looked and stared in wonder at "Mr. Luke's new spyglass."

Henry told him, "I've never seen nothin' like this. Mebbe you should get your ma to help. I dunno little picky stuff like this 'tall."

Consequently, it was Dolly who came and read the directions to her son while Luke did the actual work of putting the telescope together and getting it ready for some night-viewing.

"Isn't it a beauty?" he marveled and carried it into his cottage where it would be safe until darkness came. The telescope had come with software so he could find out what to look for and which section of the sky to look at. He studied that carefully most of the day. He set the date on the software for August 8, 2008, and made notes on where and for what he would search that night.

After dinner, he set up a folding chair and his telescope out in the middle of the grass where it would be especially dark even if people left a light on in the house – which, of course, they had been strictly forbidden to do. He also took a little collapsible table, his star map, a tiny Maglight flashlight, and a couple of cans of Coke with him. He was all set up ... except that his mother brought him a jacket for when it got cold later.

He could hardly wait. He thought the sun would <u>never</u> go down, but it finally did. He first looked long and hard at the first quarter moon. He could see the Sea of Tranquility where the astronauts had first landed. He felt like he could reach out and touch it. He went and woke up his mom and made her come down and look – which she did in her pj's and slippers. She made the proper remarks and went back to bed.  Meanwhile, Luke turned his telescope to the west where he could see Scorpio. Sagittarius was in the south just to the left of Scorpio. He could just make out

Neptune in Capricorn, but he would have to wait patiently for Uranus to rise. He sat there patiently.

He smelled it before he saw it. He sat very, very still, and watched as a big skunk toddled slowly past him. The skunk didn't seem to mind that he was there, and Luke didn't care about the skunk as long as it kept going.

Elsewhere in the world while Luke was innocently looking at the stars and the planets, evil was afoot in the area, and a nightmare was upon them. The next morning the sheriff came by to talk to André and the others.

Much to everyone's dismay, the sheriff told them that sometime around midnight last night, Cloud had been attacked, beaten badly, and raped. She was in the hospital in critical condition – having several broken bones and a bad contusion to the head.

All of the women immediately piled into Dolly's Forester for the drive to town to be with Cloud in the hospital. At the same time, the sheriff wanted to question the men who lived there to see if they could give him any information or any leads about what may have happened. He said he'd talk to them one by one. Dolly protested that Luke should go with the women.

She informed the sheriff, "He's only twelve, and you can't question him unless I'm present. He's going with me!" Naturally, she got her way. She usually did. After the women and Luke had driven away, the sheriff talked first to André: "Cloud works here for you I understand. What time did she leave last night?"

"Good grief, I don't know. Let me think. I don't think it was one of her cooking nights – they all take turns you see. She may have left before dinner. No, wait a minute. I think she had dinner with us because I remember her talking at the table about her reading."

"What'd she say?"

"She said she liked the words 'quibbling' and 'weaseling' – new words to her, and she liked the sound of them. She was reading something English, I think. Everything she reads fascinates her."

"Did she say anything about where she goes after work or whether she had a date or was meeting somebody?" the sheriff asked.

"No. I don't think she ever talked about her private life – at least not to me," André answered. "Now, she may have talked more to the girls, but she had kind of an attitude about men, I think"

"What kind of attitude?"

"Oh, you know. The modern feminine thing – that all men are no damned good – that all sex is rape. I'm not sure. She just seemed so have a haughty way about her."

"Hmmm. I see," the sheriff said. "So do you think she would report any old sex as being rape? Is that what you're implying here?"

"No. Not at all. That's not what I meant. I'm sure if she says she was raped, she was raped," André answered.

"Okay, then. Is Henry around here today? Can I talk to him?"

"Well, yeah, he's here somewhere. I'll round him up while you talk to Robert if you want to."

"Oh, and one more thing, André. Where were you last night?"

"I was in my study … my studio … whatever you want to call it. I was watching my grandson from my window as he used his new telescope to study the stars," André paused, "And no, no one saw me there. I kept the lights out so they wouldn't interfere with Luke's star searching."

Very shortly Robert came to the sheriff to be questioned. No doubt André had spoken to him and told him what all the questions would entail.

Robert started in immediately, "She left shortly after dinner – which would have been about 7:00 or 7:30. And I was here in my cottage with the lights off so I wouldn't interfere with Luke's telescope thing. But I did have the television on and was alternately watching and nodding off all evening. I watched until after Jay Leno finished making fun of all the political candidates and then I turned the thing off. I can't believe that the Democrats might actually run a woman, can you?"

The sheriff shifted gears a bit and said, "So how did you feel about Cloud? And by the way, I try to stay non-political except at election time, Mr. Liú. It is Mr. Liú, isn't it?"

"Well, to be completely politically correct, it's Mr. Fung-Liú, but I'd appreciate it if you'd call me Robert. It seems more friendly and less threatening." Robert said, "How'd I feel about Cloud? She was André's household and helper, wasn't she? I didn't feel anything about her. I saw her here, there, and everywhere working around the place. She did a lot of the cooking. And she was working on a reading list that

André had given her to improve her education. But other than that I don't know anything about her. I tried to ignore her as much as possible. She is sort of touchy and not very friendly. I think she doesn't like men … may be a lesbian, I don't know for sure."

"And, Mr. Liú … Robert … how do you feel about lesbians?" the sheriff quickly asked.

"Damned waste. Other than that, I don't care what people do or don't do with their lives. I have enough trouble trying to run my own life."

"You have a record, Mr. Liú?"

"No. Well, yes, but nothing major and certainly nothing in Oregon or at any time in the last ten years or so. I've aged into a mellow law-abiding citizen, sheriff. You should be looking at the people in town – the ones who were spreading rumors about André starting a commune or cult or something out here. Henry told us that there were stories going around all over town."

"I will talk to Henry shortly, and I'll ask him about that. Meanwhile, don't plan to leave Oregon until this is cleared up. Is that clear, Mr. Liú … Robert?"

Robert went off mumbling profanity under his breath. He went back to his cottage and turned on the television so he'd have something else to think about just as André went by leading Henry to talk to the sheriff.

"Hello, Henry," the sheriff said, "How've you been?"

"I reckon I'm doin' fine, Mr. Melville. I got no complaints," Henry answered.

Henry and the sheriff both leaned against the county car, and the sheriff asked, " Now, Henry, have you heard what's going on? Do you know why I'm here this morning? And why I'm asking people questions?"

"Mr. André said that somebody hurt Miss Cloud and that you want to find out who did it," Henry answered.

"Yes, that's right, Henry. Fact is that somebody damned near killed the poor girl and raped her. She's in really bad shape in the hospital. Do you know anything about this, Henry?"

Henry had jumped back and held himself in an anxiously tight little hug when the Sheriff said the word "rape" and he now said, "Oh Lord help us! No. I never. I wouldn't never do nothing to hurt Miss Cloud. That's ugly and awful! Who would want to do such an nasty-mean thing?" Henry grew red in the face, and he began to ball up his fists as if he would fight someone.

"Easy. Easy there, Henry. Don't you worry. I'll find out who did this and put them away in jail for a good long time. But let me ask you a couple more things first."

"Okay, Mr. Melville."

"Henry, I need you to tell me where you were last night – late. And I need you to tell me about the back-fence talk that you've been hearing around about town."

"Okay, Mr. Melville. Let's see. I was at home last night. Yup, I was sound asleep. I recollect that I had a bad dream and got up once to pee, but I slept good in spite of having a big dill pickle right before bed."

"And what about the talk around town, Henry?"

"Well, Gerry down to the café asked me about that. She told me about it at first. She gives me free pie when I tell her what's going on out here – free ice cream with it, too. You won't tell Mr. André, will you? I don't reckon he'd like that very much."

"No I won't tell him, Henry. Now, go on with your story about what you've heard."

"Well, Gerry said that people were saying that Mr. André was setting up a cult of commies and lezbos out here. I don't know what lezbos are. But she did say that having a couple of Chinks out here was a sure sign of Communism. I guess she meant Mr. Robert and Mrs. Joy, didn't she? But I don't think they are communists. I've never actually seen a communist, but I think I'd know one when I saw one. She said that one of the folks here is a Jew and that all of the women with the real short hair were sure signs of somethin' or another. I told her when they were puttin' in the new bathroom and the new stairs, but there wasn't much else going on that I know of … Oh! Oh! I should have told her about that new spyglass that Luke has. He was lookin' at something last night … or at least he was settin' up to when I left for the day. He said he would be able to see the moon real clear and other stuff, but I dunno what else he does with it."

"Okay, Henry, now you go back to whatever chores André has you doing today. If I need to talk to you again, I'll be in touch. Meanwhile, stop telling Gerry anything you see or hear out here. I'll talk to her and you'll still get your free pie and ice cream. I promise you that, but just don't tell her anything more."

Henry pulled off his gloves and shook hands with the sheriff and then wandered on back out to the gardens where he was dead-heading the roses today – at least the ones that the deer hadn't eaten.

André came back out of the house to tell the sheriff that he and Robert were going to go to town now to see Cloud, and the sheriff left as well.

The sheriff drove directly to Gerry's Diner. As soon as he had his coffee in front of him, he confronted her, "Now, Gerry, why aren't you over at the hospital seeing to Cloud? She's your kin, isn't she?"

"Sure. She's my sister's kid, and I would be over there, but who'd run the café? She knows – she gets it that I can't leave the café or I don't make any money today, and the cook might leave if he didn't have a day's income today. She knows." Gerry said, "And I'll go over after I close up and spend time with her."

"She lives with you, does she?"

"Yeah, she has a room at my house, but she spends her days out at André's place. I bet anything it was hanging around with those creepy people that got her in trouble."

"Creepy? Creepy how?" Sheriff Melville asked.

"Oh, you must have heard…it's some kind of commune or cult kind of deal with lesbians and commies and Jews."

"Well, Gerry, I think you're mistaken. Those people are just André's family – an assorted sort of family, but family nonetheless. And I want you to stop spreading rumors about those folks. I told Henry not to tell you anything that goes on out there – ever again. But I also told him that you'd still give him free pie and ice cream. So here's a twenty. Make sure to keep him happy because I'll hear about it if you don't. When you run out of that twenty dollars, just let me know. And now, do I need a warrant to go to your place and search Cloud's room?"

"No. 'Course not. Go on with ya."

18. Bruises, Bandages & Bad Guys

Cloud was still in Intensive Care when the women got to the hospital – so they could visit her only one at a time. And the nurse said only family could visit.

Joy assured her, "We're all family here." And she went in first. Cloud was asleep with a respirator rhythmically pumping air through a tube in her mouth plus an automatic heart, blood pressure, and pulse monitor. Her head was bandaged, and she had a cast on her left leg. Ugly bruises showed on her arms and on the part of her face that Joy could see.

Joy sat in the one chair next to the bed and held Cloud's hand. She said, "I can only stay a minute because everyone else wants to say 'hello' to you, too. I just want you to know that we are here with you in every way. You are family to us." Joy paused and wiped away some tears, "You didn't deserve this, Cloud. You have good karma and a very favorable aura. Someone very evil did this to you, and I hope they get what's coming to them."

Joy went back out to the waiting room still wiping tears from her eyes. Miki embraced her and then was next into Cloud's room.

Miki's reaction was to immediately kneel down next to the bed and offer a prayer for Cloud's recovery. She said, "Mother Mary pray for us." Then she went on, "Lord, You invite all who are burdened to come to you. Allow Your healing Hand to heal Cloud. Touch her soul with Your compassion for others; touch her heart with Your courage and infinite Love for all; touch her mind with Your Wisdom.

"May my mouth always proclaim Your praise. Teach me to reach out to You in all my needs, and help me to lead others to You by my example.

"Most loving Heart of Jesus, bring Cloud health in body and spirit that she may serve You with all her strength. Touch gently this life which you have created, now and forever. Amen."[viii]

Miki pulled herself up slowly from her knees. She told Cloud, "It's not as easy to get up off the floor as it used to be. Ha! Now, Cloud, I think you know that we all love you and depend on you. We will all pray for you and will be here for you through all of this. When you wake up, we will be right here."

Miki left the room as Dolly slipped in and Dolly gasped as she saw the terrible picture before her. "Oh God, who could have done such a thing as this? I expect to see something like this in Los Angeles or maybe Oakland down in California, but not here. This place seems so safe – so secure. I suppose there is evil everywhere, and we need to be more watchful and more careful. Oh, Cloud, I am sorry that this had to happen to you. In spite of your studs and tattoo and put-on attitudes, I know you are a sweet, innocent girl. I will – we all will – do whatever we can to help you heal. And we will all pray for you."

Dolly asked Luke if he wanted to go in, but he didn't think he wanted to see Cloud just then. So they all sat down and looked around for a magazine to read that was less than a year old. Joy suggested coffee or tea for everyone, and Luke was sent as their gofer to find the cafeteria and bring back: one tea with sugar or honey only, one coffee with cream and sugar, and one black coffee – plus whatever he wanted for himself.

The women sat there looking out the window, back at the nurse's station, and everywhere except at each other. Finally, Miki could stand the silence no longer.

"You guys, I know we are a very strange family, but we <u>are</u> a family. And we should talk to each other and get to know each other. I mean, look at poor Cloud, bless her heart …you just never know what's going to happen, do you?"

Joy smiled and responded, "You are absolutely right, Miki. Just consider us … we are as different as night and day and well, whatever. I mean, there are huge contrasts. We are of different ages – different decades even. We are of different religions and different ethnicity. But it appears that we are family."

Dolly said, "We are probably the <u>most</u> dysfunctional family ever, but we need to stick together and be sisters if we can. I know Luke likes both of you, and he thinks of you as Aunt Joy and Aunt Miki. Of course, the dogs were a good ice breaker for him. He and I have been alone since my husband died. He visits his grandparents from time to time, but that's not the same as having family close by."

Miki said, "I never really had much of a family. I was raised by my grandparents. My mother is a Nun. Can you imagine? You would never have guessed, would you? Well, anyway, my family was mostly my roommates – two really amazing guys. They were like my brothers. I miss them very much. And, of course, I have my dogs who are my children, but it would be good to have the two of you as pseudo-sisters and Luke as a terrific nephew."

Luke came back into the room with the coffee and tea just in time to hear Miki call him a nephew. He smiled widely and said, "Thanks, Auntie Miki."

"Oh, let's just make it Miki, shall we?" Miki said as she hugged him.

He said, "I just saw André and Robert coming this way. I guess the sheriff finished questioning them."

André came around the corner to the nurse's station and demanded to see Cloud and to see the doctor in charge of her case. Naturally, the nurse went through the story again of only one person at a time and only family being allowed.

André harrumphed and sternly said that he <u>was</u> family and again demanded to see the doctor. Meanwhile, he ducked into Cloud's room where everyone saw him hold her hand.

He told her, "Cloud, my god, Cloud. I am so sorry for what has happened to you. I hope to Hell it didn't have anything to do with you working for me. I know some of the folks around here resent me ... probably still blame me for Vivienne's death. But I can tell you this, my dear, if I find out who did this to you, I'll kill him!"

The doctor had been paged and was in the

waiting room with Joy, Miki, Dolly, Luke, and Robert when André came back out of Cloud's room. André introduced himself and asked the doctor, "What's her condition? Is she going to be all right?"

The doctor seemed like a very young man to André and he wasn't sure he could be trusted with Cloud's care. But the doctor said, "She's had some real trauma which is why I have her drugged right now. I didn't want her to wake up until her leg was set and some of her other injuries were sutured. She's also had an MRI of her brain to see if there were any injuries from the knock on the head, but it appears it's a concussion only. That's bad enough, but at least there is no internal bleeding there."

"Well, when can we take her home?" André asked.

"Not for awhile yet. Many of her injuries are where you cannot see them. She has a couple of broken ribs that are going to hurt every time she breathes, but the worst part is internal. She may need surgery, I'm afraid. I've called a gynecologist to check her, but I think it's possible that she may lose all or part of her reproductive organs," Dr. Scott said calmly.

"Oh no! Oh god! Oh Hell!" Miki and the other women all cried at once. "She is so young," Miki continued, "She should have the opportunity to have a family. This is tragic."

"Well," the doctor said, "don't get all upset yet. Like I said, I've called in a specialist. Let's wait until she has a chance to examine the patient before we jump to any conclusions."

"Thank you, Doctor Scott. We appreciate everything you are doing for Cloud. She is very important to us," Joy said.

André broke in, "How old are you anyway? Where did you go to medical school? Do you have the experience to take care of Cloud or do I need to bring in someone from Portland?"

The doctor chuckled and said, "Mr. Zhalovy, I assure you that I have been practicing medicine, especially trauma room medicine, for a number of years. I graduated from the University of Colorado Medical School in Denver more years ago than you think. You can see my diploma and other certificates in my office if you like. But you are always free to call in another doctor at any time."

"No. No, I guess you're okay," André said. "I'm just old, and everybody looks like a kid to me these days. So forgive me and don't pay any attention to me. Just do whatever Cloud needs – no worries – I'll pay for it."

"We'll be waking her up soon. It will be better for her to be examined by the GYN while she's awake and aware. I guess you all will still be here then?"

"You bet we will!" André exclaimed.

Sheriff Melville joined them in the waiting room. He said, "I gotta talk to her first when she wakes up. Dr. Scott called to say that they're getting ready to bring her around about now."

"Any clues yet, sheriff?" André asked.

"No. Not really. I searched her room at Gerry's house. Nothing there that one wouldn't expect to find … no drugs, no drug paraphernalia. I did find a book that she appeared to be reading along with a dictionary, both at the side of her bed. And some candy bar wrappers in the trash, but nothing of any interest. You know, though, it occurred to me that the room was awfully small, dark, and uncomfortable. Maybe you should think about moving her out to your place once she's well enough. You got a another room available?"

André answered, "I can make room. I'll put my stuff in the studio. I don't need to be taking up two rooms."

"Or Luke could move in with me," Dolly offered.

"Oh, Mom!" Luke cried.

"Well, in any case, we'll make a nice room for her," Joy said. "She should be with us, shouldn't she?"

Everybody agreed. Then they saw the doctor and two nurses fussing with Cloud in her room. The sheriff walked over to the door and watched what was happening and then slipped into the room.

The doctor told him he could talk to Cloud for a few minutes only, "And please don't upset her."

"I'll try," Sheriff Melville said, "But I have to ask … Cloud, do you know who did this to you? Did you get a good look at whoever beat you and assaulted you?"

Cloud blinked her eyes and whimpered softly, "Yeah, I saw them."

"Them? Who? Who was it, Cloud?" the sheriff asked softly.

"The Cunningham brothers," Cloud murmured, "both of them."

"Did both of them beat you?"

"Yeah."

"Did both of them rape you, Cloud?"

"Yeah. Both."

"Thank you, Cloud. Don't worry. I'll take care of this. You just rest and get better. You have a bunch of people who care about you, you know."

The sheriff came back out of the room. André quickly accosted him and wanted to know exactly what

Cloud had told him, but Sheriff Melville just kept walking and left the family there to watch as a lady doctor entered Cloud's room and all the blinds were drawn during her examination.

The women held hands and the men paced back and forth for what seemed like a very long time. Finally, both doctors emerged, leaving the nurses to make Cloud comfortable and to give her some juice to drink.

"I think we may be lucky," Dr. Scott said.

"Yes. Uh, hello, my name is Dr. Wagner. I've just examined your … Cloud. I think I will be able to reconstruct the damage that was done. It will be tricky, but I don't think the damage will be permanent."

"Oh, that's wonderful," Miki said.

"Yes, that's great." "Thank heaven." The others all said.

"I can operate first thing in the morning. Dr. Scott will assist me, and I think we'll have your … what is she anyway? Your daughter? Your sister?"

"She's our sister," Dolly said, "and how long do you think she'll be hospitalized."

"If all goes well, it should just be something like three to five days," Dr. Wagner said.

"But," Dr. Scott added, "her recovery will take a lot longer than that. She will need people to help her get around, and she may need counseling to help with the trauma of the whole thing. After all it's been a terrible shock to her."

André said, "I understand. I'll take care of whatever she needs. Can we go in to see her now?"

"Actually, the nurses are getting ready to move her to the surgical ward which is on the second floor, south wing. Why don't you all head over that way and you can see her there."

19. August Heat

The sheriff soon caught up with the Cunningham brothers. They drove a huge cherry red Ford F-350 with orange flames painted on the front and sides, American flags flying from both sides and a .22 rifle permanently placed in the back window. Fact is, they would have been hard to miss. The sheriff pulled them over as they were cruising down Main Street.

The sheriff asked Don and Gary, "Do you know why I stopped you?"

Don said, "I can't rightly reckon. We wasn't speedin' or nothin'."

Sheriff Melville asked them, "Do you know Gerry's niece, Cloud?"

"Sure. Everybody 'knows' Cloud." And both men snickered.

"Where were you boys last night – around midnight?" the sheriff asked.

"At home watching TV with our mama," Don said, and Gary nodded his head in agreement.

"Well, boys I'm sorry to tell you this, but I have a very good witness who says you were not at home … that you were, in fact, busy beating and raping Cloud. So I guess I'm gonna have to arrest you both and take you into the jail – on charges of kidnapping, assault, and rape."

The sheriff had previously called for police backup and the cops who had been standing by pulled the two big fellows out of their shiny red truck, read them their rights, and asked if they understood those rights while putting cuffs on both of them.

Don hollered, "Look here, Sheriff Melville, the bitch is lying to you. We never forced her. She wanted it … wanted it bad! And we never beat her up neither. She fell down a few times because she was drunk or something."

And Gary offered, "Besides that, she had it comin'. She's just a damned lezbo livin' out there with them other commies and lezbos."

"So you didn't do it, but if you had done it, she would have had it coming. Is that right?" the sheriff asked.

"Yeah!" Gary said, "That's right, isn't it, Don?"

"Oh, just shut up, Gary!"

The rumors about the folks out at André's place died down at least temporarily after the Cunningham boys' arrest.

Back at the house, André moved into his studio. Cloud was ensconced in his old bedroom (after Joy redecorated it). Cloud recovered little by little. Luke started school. Dolly started work on the forested land. Her birthday passed without notice except from Luke who gave her a balloon bouquet and a big box of dark chocolates. Miki took lots of pictures. Joy played the piano and started writing her book. The Cunningham brothers were imprisoned after they both finally pleaded guilty to all charges. Robert continued giving everyone cooking lessons until he met a woman who interested him.

Moving André had been no big thing. He just bought another bed, had it brought in, and took all of his clothes and things to the closets and bathroom connected to his studio. It was a little crowded for him compared to what he'd been used to, but he said he could handle it.

Joy and Miki went into his old room and scrubbed everything down as if there had been a gang of homeless people camping out in there. They painted the walls a nice green – called "Jaded Lime" which was supposed to be soothing, and put in new white curtains, towels, and bedding. When Cloud could come home, Robert and Henry made a chair of their arms and carried her up to her new room. She was surprised and pleased to find her own clothes and other necessities already in place – along with the book she had been reading and her dictionary right next to the bed.

Her leg was now in a walking cast so she could get up and take herself to the bathroom, but she was still very sore and needed people to bring her meals to her because she couldn't manage the stairs. When he was around, Robert usually carried her meals up to her. He said it was the least he could do for her. She finished reading To Kill a Mockingbird and exclaimed that it must be the very best book ever written. Miki gave her a copy of Pride and Prejudice and asked her to let her know how she liked that one.

Everyone had to sign Cloud's new cast. They had written on the one she wore before, and they couldn't very well leave this one all white and pristine. So they wrote things like: *"Tough Break!" "Busted!"* and *"Don't fall to pieces!"* They each used a different colored pen – and Miki drew flowers here and there as well.

Getting Luke started in school wasn't as difficult as Dolly had feared it might be. She got his school records from Yreka and took them to the high school where he was to be a freshman. He signed up for the classes that were expected for a ninth grade student:

English, Algebra, World History, and Biology. To that he added a Spanish class, and asked if he could go out for football. Dolly was as fearful about football injuries as any mother would be, but she gave in when she saw the urgent look on his face day after day.

Dolly hired a contractor to come in and put a rudimentary road into the forest land and then with a big Cat began clearing the dead wood and the undergrowth. The contractor got any good wood on the road right-of-way as payment for putting in the road. But the small, ugly stuff was just hauled down near the main highway so people could pick it up. During the fire season, they couldn't burn anything, but this would make good firewood for the winter and the price was right: Free! As the contractor got the land cleared, they started spraying herbicides. This was a licensed contractor who did the job, and he was very careful.

When Miki learned that Dolly actually planned to cut some of the trees, she had a conniption! She said, "Don't you care anything about the environment? Don't you know anything about conservation?"

To this tirade Dolly calmly answered, "I have read many definitions of what is a conservationist, and I have actually written a few myself, but I suspect the best one is written not

with a pen, but with an axe. It is a matter of what a person thinks about while chopping or deciding where to chop. A conservationist is one who is humbly aware that with each stroke he is writing his signature on the face of the land.[ix] The forest will be healthier once it is thinned."

Miki took many pictures of nature like the ones shown here. And she rejoiced as her Democrat Party nominated Barack Hussein Obama for the Presidential election at their

convention in August. She was joined in her admiration by Robert, but all the others were disappointed and said that either they had wanted Mrs.

Clinton – or they wanted a Republican. But it was all sort of friendly, family-style debate – no ranting allowed. When the Republican Party nominated John McCain, there was some disappointment because of his age and the fact that he wasn't conservative enough, but the disappointment was soon turned to rejoicing when he asked Sarah Palin to be his running mate. They were all able to agree that she was an "inspired" choice for Vice President

Henry came unglued when he heard that Dolly was using herbicides in the forest. He told her, "I always pull the weeds in the garden. I never ever use those weed killers. They're poison! Very bad."

Dolly countered with, "Yes, well Henry, we're not using weed killers like you find at the Home Store. We're using proper "herbicides.""

Henry thought about that for awhile and then said, "Well, then I guess that's okay."

Joy played the piano whenever she was alone in the house. She didn't play as well as she once had. She didn't play as well as she thought she should, but she enjoyed the lovely sound anyway. It was a very good piano and had a very mellow tone – as well it should – it was a Baldwin baby grand. She played mostly classical music – some Chopin, Bach, Rachmaninoff, and Beethoven, but she also played some show tunes and ordered sheet music online to increase her repertoire. She also got out her laptop and started writing a book about her experiences growing up as a Chinese-American who knew that her mother had committed suicide but not knowing at all who her father was. Now that she knew, it gave her the little push she needed to get started.

Everyone was so glad when the Cunningham brothers, Don and Gary, made a deal with the prosecutor and took the plea bargain that would put them each in jail for twelve years each whereas they could have gotten as much as twenty-five if a jury found them guilty on all charges. This was good because it meant that Cloud wouldn't have to testify and relive all that trauma in a courtroom.

Robert met a woman through an online dating service. She was from Eugene, which was quite a drive to make very often, but she was younger than Robert and better looking, too. The fact that she had money of her own was also very attractive, and Robert found it necessary to spend a lot of time in Eugene that month. André told Cloud that if Robert moved out, she could have his cottage and then she wouldn't have to worry about the stairs. But in the meantime, nobody wanted Robert to sleep in the house because his snoring was unbelievably loud. Luke concluded that the noise kept the bears and cougars away. After all, until the rainy season started, Luke was still out almost every night looking at the stars, and he could hear Robert's snorting and snuffling very distinctly. Luke guessed he'd never heard a bear, but still this must be somewhat similar.

20. Fall

The deciduous trees turned their leaves to various lovely shades of yellow, orange, and red while the mighty fir and pine stood guard for the winter ahead.

The women now had regular get-togethers to just talk about whatever was on their minds. At first they always met in Cloud's room, but soon they moved the talks to various restaurants in town where they could have a nice lunch and a good conversation.

People in town still stared at them. There were still rumors in abundance, but the women were treated politely – if not warmly.

One time, sitting at the table in The Fish House, Miki said, "You know, I don't think we've ever talked about our love lives. How can that be? Four women should be talking about men and love and stuff like that."

Joy said, "That's because none of us has a love life, Miki, and I personally don't want one."

"Why not?"

"Well, I've been married three times ... and had a few lovers in between. None of them gave me any happiness – well, except for the first one who gave me two beautiful children. So why would I want a man in my life?"

"Yeah," Dolly said, "I understand completely how you feel. I'm still in my thirties – and should be looking around, I suppose. But I married the one love of my life and once he was gone, I guess I just didn't feel like kissing a bunch of frogs looking for another prince."

"Kissing frogs! I like that," Cloud said. "And that's about all you'll find around here – frogs, toads, and other ugly, creepy things."

"Oh, Cloud, I'm sorry to bring this up. I shouldn't have, should I? It was insensitive of me," Miki said.

"No, not at all, Miki. Life goes on – and look at me – I don't even have any bruises left," Cloud said.

"Maybe not on the outside, Cloud, but … well, what can I say? See, the thing is that I've never had a real relationship. I guess it's because (one) I'm a little fat and (two) I'm Catholic – the first kept the men away and the second kept me chaste." Everyone laughed lightly and politely. "But, you know, I keep thinking about that veterinarian, Dr. Wayne. He was so gentle with the dogs. I was attracted to him, you know."

"Well then," said Joy, "we need to find out whether he's single and if so, you need to make another appointment to take in one of the dogs."

"Neither one of them is sick or anything."

"Oh, we won't let that stop you, will we, girls?"

Cloud immediately opened her little cell phone and made a quick call, "Hi, Aunt Gerry, this is Cloud. Yes. Yes, I'm fine. No. I'm not over-doing anything. Everyone is helping me. You don't need to worry. But, hey, I do have a question. You know everyone in town, right? Yeah. Well, do you know Dr. Wayne, the vet? Yeah. Uh-huh. Well, is he married or spoken for or anything? Uh-huh. Okay. Oh, no reason, I just wondered. Thanks, Aunt Gerry … see you soon." And she flipped her little phone closed.

"Well? Well, what did she say?"

"She said that he's divorced. His wife left him a few years back, and he's lived alone out there over the clinic ever since."

"Whoopee!" Joy said, "Now, all we have to do is make a plan to get Miki out there to see him and get her to loosen up her tongue long enough to ask him out for coffee or something."

Miki had turned all shades of red during this conversation and now said, "I don't think I can do this."

"Of course, you can. We'll practice. But first we need to find a reason to take one of the dogs out there."

Miki quickly added, "And it can't be something gross that would hurt them."

"How about just a general check up. Do they do that for dogs? They do it for people. I don't know why they wouldn't do it for dogs."

Miki said, "I could tell him that I'm worried about Punkin being lethargic or something like that, I guess. But that's nothing new. She sleeps most of time anyway."

"Well, he doesn't know that," Joy said, "Go ahead and call him up and make an appointment."

"Now?"

"What better time than now?"

"Well, okay, I guess." Miki said and extracted her own little cell phone from her handbag. She had the vet's number stored in her contact list and she was quickly connected with the veterinarian office. "Hello. Yes, hello, this is Miki Miller calling. I wanted to make an appointment to see Dr. Wayne about my little dog, Punkin. No, it's not an emergency. I just want him to check on her. She has seemed so lethargic lately. Yes, I know that's not unusual in the hot weather, but, well, I am worried about her, you see. Right. Okay. I can come in any time that's convenient for the doctor. Yes.

Tomorrow morning at 11:00 would be fine. Yes, Punkin and I will be there. Thank you." And she took a long breath and exhaled slowly as she finally hit the "end" button and put the phone back in her bag.

"Jeeze Louise! That's like lying to one of the Sisters," Miki said. "I've never been so nervous."

"Well, you can go to confession on Sunday, but in the meantime ... we're proud of you!" said Dolly.

"Yes, you have taken the bull by the horns, as they say ... now let's see if you can lead him to water or whatever."

The next day all four women were in Miki's cottage helping her decide what to wear. It's not an easy choice to decide what to wear to a vet appointment – that is, if the vet appointment is only an excuse for something more. So they went through all of Miki's closet and finally settled on a long aqua skirt and shirt combination. The color was very good for her, and she even happened to have earrings that matched. Not having much in the way of choice of shoes, they settled on Birkenstocks.

But Joy sternly said, "We have <u>got</u> to get you downtown and do some shopping. You just simply have <u>nothing</u> to wear. Suppose he asks you out to dinner? My god, sweetheart, you have got to have something nice – at least one little black dress and maybe a red one. Yes, or blue. Royal blue would look good on you, I think. And that would require new shoes. Oh heavens, I will make a list and we'll go tomorrow."

Dolly whispered to Cloud, "Joy is enjoying this. She will have a wonderful time shopping for Miki. Maybe I should let her look in my closet?" And then out loud to Miki she said, "Take the Forester. I'm not going to be using it today, and it is much more dependable than your old Volvo."

"Thanks. Thanks everyone. I'm nervous as a cat. I'm sure Punkin will pick up on that. She'll probably be very scared at the vet's office – and she's a drama queen anyway. She'll shake like a leaf," Miki said.

"Well, that way, he won't notice you're shaking."

When the time came Miki loaded Punkin into the Forester and left Denzel with Luke. Denzel had been getting into the pool and from there into the house again, and it was driving them all wild. So Luke was trying to teach him not to do that because people didn't like wet dogs shaking all over all the furniture.

Miki arrived at the Veterinarian Clinic right on time and gave the receptionist all the information she had on Punkin – which was kept neatly in a folder – records of shots and exams but not much else because Punkin had never been sick since Miki got her. They waited – Miki shaking a little and Punkin quaking as if she were being led to the guillotine – but they didn't have long to wait.

Dr. Wayne came out and greeted them and put Punkin on the scale where he announced that she weighed fourteen pounds, which was just about right for her breed and age. Then they went together into the examination room.

Dr. Wayne asked, "So tell me what we can do for this little lady today."

Miki said nervously, "Oh, I just thought she'd been lethargic lately and maybe should have a check up. You can just check her over. Right?"

"Well, of course, I can. She's a very pretty little Shih Tzu. Let's see here … hmmm … good teeth, bright eyes, good musculature. Let me listen to her heart. Uh-huh. Sounds good. You say she's been lethargic?"

"Uh, yes, a little bit less active than usual I would say." Miki answered.

"Well, it's probably just the hot weather we're having. Let me draw some blood though just to make sure." The vet left the room for a couple of minutes with Punkin. When he came back, he said, "Try to take her out on walks first thing in the morning. Let's see here … yes, you are also the owner of Denzel the beautiful Labrador, right?"

"Yes, right."

"Well, take the two of them out together first thing in the morning before it gets sunny and hot, and then just keep them inside during the heat of the day. She looks fine to me. Nothing to worry about. I'll let you know about the results of the blood tests, but I don't expect to see any problem."

"Oh good," Miki said.

"Any other questions I can answer for you?"

"Um, yes, Dr. Wayne … would you go out with me for coffee or lunch or something sometime?" Miki spit it out as fast as she could before she lost her nerve.

Dr. Wayne looked a bit surprised but said, "Why, yes, I'd enjoy that very much Miss Miller."

"Oh do please call me Miki – everyone does. It's short for Mary Katherine."

"When shall we have coffee or lunch, Miki?"

"Well, just whenever is good for you. I'm sure you're busier than I am. You just name the time and place," Miki answered.

"How about I pick you up at André's house so you don't have to drive all the way to town alone? And I'll come tomorrow at about noon … if that's okay with you?"

"That's fine. That's wonderful. Thank you." Miki picked up Punkin and carried her to the car – at which point she remembered to double back and pay for the examination. She was a little embarrassed about forgetting such a thing, but the receptionist didn't even seem to notice.

And so the two of them met the next day – after Joy had rushed to town to buy Miki something to wear – this time a colorful peasant skirt and white blouse with white sandals and a long string of red beads. The lunch went very well. They talked and talked – until Dr. Wayne had to get back to the Clinic, but he assured her that he would definitely call … which he did that same night and most every night after that.

October arrived, and Dolly declared, "I sometimes think that the other months are constituted as a fitting interlude between Octobers. The weather is so beautiful in October."

O suns and skies and clouds of June,
And flowers of June together,
Ye cannot rival for one hour
October's bright blue weather…
~Helen Hunt Jackson [x]

October is the month of the start of the rainy season in Oregon, but the fine weather usually holds out until mid-October. And when it finally comes, the rain is very welcome. The hills have been very thirsty all summer, and the rain soaks in and feeds the grasses and the trees. The flowers fade and fall. The roses give their last gasp of bloom and frost comes to the pumpkin fields. Children buy them to make Jack-o-lanterns but most of them go for cattle food or to feed the elephants in the zoo.

Henry put a big insulated cover over the swimming pool inside and out, and did what he thought was necessary to protect the gardens through the winter. Some of his flowers were annuals and would need replanting in any case, but he did try to save the geraniums and some of the other perennials. He also replanted the big bucketful of daffodil bulbs that he had dug up earlier in the year. Other than that, there wasn't much work around the place for Henry. He did chop a lot of fire wood for Mr. Zhalovy from the supply that had dried out and weathered since last year, but when he finished with that Mr. Zhalovy said he might was well "move along" until next summer.

Henry was, at first, a bit confused. The women had told him he was part of the family. He shouldn't just be discarded like that, should he? But Robert promised to talk to Mr. Zhalovy about the problem, and Henry went away – to wherever he lived – and to Gerry's Diner for pie and ice cream even in the winter.

Luke was invited to a Halloween party by his new high school friends. Dolly, Miki, and Joy all worked on making his costume so that he could go dressed as an astronaut – specifically Buzz Aldrin, Luke insisted. They did the best they could, and Luke was a big hit at the party.

Other than that, October might have passed peacefully and unnoticed except that as soon as it became apparent that the nation was about to elect

Barack Obama as president, the stock market took a **dive**. All of the indexes fell abruptly and continued to fall. People, including André, were suddenly about half as rich as they thought they were. Though some of his money (Vivienne's actually) was in protected accounts, a great portion of it was in the market and shrank right along with everyone else's.

21. The Melancholy of November

"How silently they tumble down
And come to rest upon the ground
To lay a carpet, rich and rare,
Beneath the trees without a care,
Content to sleep, their work well done,
Colors gleaming in the sun.

At other times, they wildly fly
Until they nearly reach the sky.
Twisting, turning through the air
Till all the trees stand stark and bare.
Exhausted, drop to earth below
To wait, like children, for the snow."
~ Elsie N. Brady, *Leaves* ~[xi]

October turned to November with little notice. The election went exactly the way everyone thought it would, and the stock market continued its downward trend. André talked to everyone about the change in their financial circumstances. All were willing to cut back if necessary, but none seemed to really mind because nothing much changed for them. They did express concern about the danger of extraordinary costs – like major medical expenses. However, they noticed little difference except the weather, which was gray and dreary much of the time. For the first time they had a fire in the fireplace and sat near it in the evening for warmth and for company.

Luke's birthday was quickly approaching, and Dolly was being inundated with calls from Dorothy who wanted to know what sort of arrangements had been made for his Bar Mitzvah.

Dorothy would usually say something like, "Now, Deirdre, I realize that you are not a Jew and probably have no idea how important this is to a young man. Do you want me to handle everything from here? I can easily do that for you. Is there even a Temple in town – or a Rabbi?"

As the date drew nearer, Dolly finally had to admit that there was not a Temple nor a Rabbi nearby. In fact, she eventually admitted, "I looked it up on the Internet to see what needed to be done, but when I presented it to Luke, he came undone. He says he doesn't want to be a Jew. Maybe you should talk to him. He is really against all mention of this, Dorothy."

"Oh my God! This will kill Jacob! It would kill Maxwell if he weren't already dead, and you know it. He wanted Luke raised as a Jew. I don't suppose you have even seen to his education in Jewish ritual law, tradition, and ethics, have you?"

"No, Dorothy, I have no idea how to do that, and I have been very busy seeing to his high school education and his education about people, the world, and the environment – which is all I know about for sure." Dolly answered.

"Well, let me talk to Luke," Dorothy demanded.

"He's in school right now, Dorothy. I'll have him call you later. Will that be okay?"

Dorothy said it would be fine, and both women slammed down their phones simultaneously.

The first snow came on Veteran's Day. Luke thought that was "way cool" because he didn't have to go to school anyway. The sound of the axes and the chain saws in the woods competed with the silence of the snowfall. There wasn't a lot of snow down by the house, but going up the logging road a bit they could easily get to where the snow was very impressive. They all went out to enjoy the snow. Luke and Dolly had seen snow in Yreka, but Joy, Miki, and Cloud were all thrilled with the white stuff. André watched them all out there together. At the end of the day, they were still separate and apart … still not a true family. What would it take

for him to feel like part of the group? Maybe he never would. He had wanted a family though and there they were, having fun. Maybe that was good enough? Maybe that was all he needed.

Luke was finally hounded into calling his grandmother. He said, "Hello Grandma. This is Luke. How are you?"

"How am I? How **am** I? Well, young man, how do you expect I am when your mother tells me that you want to give up your Jewish heritage. It's heart-breaking. It's tragic! You are <u>killing</u> me! You are killing your grandfather! I don't know what to tell people. What? Are you going to be a gentile now?" Dorothy yammered.

"Oh, Grandma, I don't know what I'm going to be. I just want some time and the freedom to decide for myself what I want to be. I don't know anything about being a Jew," Luke answered.

"Well, I'm sending you some books. You need to read them and study them. One is called <u>Being Jewish</u> by Ari Goldman. It's a gold mine of information. Please promise me you'll read the books I send," Dorothy implored.

"Okay, Grandma, I'll read whatever you send, and I'll let you know what I think – **if** I think anything important. But please, I want you to remember that this is not Mom's fault. She was all prepared to give me a

Bar Mitzvah even if it meant bringing in a Rabbi from Eugene or Portland."

Dolly was very proud of Luke for standing up for his rights to make his own choices. She and Dorothy could see to it that he had the information to make intelligent choices. Dolly had studied world religion as one of her classes in college, and she still had a couple of the books that Luke could look at if he wanted to. The texts covered everything from Zoroastrianism to Christianity to Buddhism to Hinduism plus everything in between. Dolly had enjoyed her these studies, and definitely helped her to find out who she was and what she believed. She hoped they would help Luke as well.

Meanwhile, in town at Gerry's Diner, Henry was becoming somewhat antsy and made it well known to whoever would listen: "Look I'm part of that family, too. They should let me live out there. Sheriff Melville says they are not commies or lezbos – so it must be okay for me to live there, too."

"Oh, Henry, you are no more a member of that family than I am," Gerry said.

"Ya-huh! Yes, I am," Henry said. "And I can prove it."

Gerry told Sheriff Melville about this the next time he came in. She said, "I think Henry is getting obsessed with that family. He told me he could **prove** that he was a member of the family."

"I'll have a talk with him, Gerry," Sheriff Melville said, "It's funny, you realize that I know everyone in town plus the names of their kids and their dogs, but I don't know where Henry lives, do you?"

"He has a shack out in the woods somewhere. That's all I know for sure," Gerry said.

"Come to think of it, Gerry, how long has Henry been around hereabout?"

"Oh years and years, I guess. I think maybe ten or fifteen years. He just showed up in town one day and started doing handy work for folks. I don't know if he has any kin here. You know, I just never thought about it before. Henry was just part of the town."

"Well, next time I see him, I'll have a talk with him. He seems like a harmless sort."

"Yeah, but he was kind of angry when he talked about not being allowed to live at Mr. Zhalovy's place."

All the while this was going on, Miki was getting a lot of beautiful snowy pictures and seeing Dr. Wayne whenever he could get away from his practice. But she also wanted to get over to the coast and take some pictures. With help from Dolly, she was able to get her old Volvo going. It needed to be driven once in awhile, Miki thought, but she was worried about driving over the coast range to get to the ocean beaches. Dolly agreed that she was worried about that as well, and offered to take Miki over in the Forester. When they heard of the plan, Joy and Cloud wanted to go, too. They would make a day of it. Cloud told them there were some really nice shops over there and some terrific art galleries. Thus, it was arranged that André would pick Luke up from school, and all the ladies were off to Bandon-by-the-Sea.

It was a beautiful drive. It took about two hours, but they enjoyed each other's company and conversation along the way. Dolly jokingly asked them all if they wanted to listen to Rush Limbaugh on the radio on the way over … she was answered with hoots, hollers, and boos. So they talked about how everyone was getting along.

Cloud said that she was so happy that the cast was coming off next week. She said her leg itched like mad, and she couldn't find anything but one of Miki's knitting needles that would reach down far enough to scratch. She also thought that probably Robert wouldn't be back. He was pretty well situated in Eugene – so maybe she could move into his cottage – or did someone else want it?

No one did. Joy said she was perfectly happy with her room now that she had it decorated – and why didn't they all come in sometime and see the beautiful silk embroidery that she had hung there? She also said that she was coming along nicely with her book plans – mostly she was just researching at this time using the Internet and André's books, but the ideas and the characters were coming together in her head so that she could get it down on paper soon.

Dolly reported that the thinning in the forest was going well and would soon be finished. "After all," she said, "it's not a huge piece of land, and we're just doing a thinning. I think you will all be surprised at how well it will do for the next twenty years or so because we thinned it this year. And," she continued, "we will be planting some baby trees in January or February in the spots that are a little bare."

Miki said, "Oh, that's wonderful. Where do you get the baby trees? Can I help with the baby trees?"

"I don't think you could even stand up on the ground where they are to be planted. It's very steep. It takes people who are accustomed to that land to do it – that and the calked boots to keep you from slipping right down the hills. I'll probably buy excess baby trees from the Bureau of Land Management and then let the contractor plant them."

At lunch time, the group drove into Old Town in

Bandon. They agreed to have lunch first and then go scouting the shops, the galleries, and the beach. Each bought a *"BANDON"* sweatshirt, and Dolly also got one for Luke. At the last minute, they went together and got one for André and Miki got one for Dr. Wayne as well. They visited the Fudge Factory and sampled every kind of fudge that was generously displayed there. Miki bought several little packages of it, but the others decided that just the

samples were enough fat and sugar for them.

They drove to the beach and got out into a cold wind that had them pulling on their brand-new sweatshirts under their jackets. They walked along the beach and marveled at how clean and pretty it was.

Miki said, "The beaches in California are always so crowded and dirty. This is beautiful! I've got to get some pictures of this. It's amazingly wild and gorgeous, isn't it? I understand that the Coast Guard trains on the Oregon Coast because it's just the wildest place there is – so much wind and such big waves. Wouldn't it be great to have a house along here some-where?"

"Well," Joy said, "I would certainly get tired of the wind in a hurry. I suppose it blows like this all the time. Don't you think so?"

"Oh, yeah, probably, but I've heard that when it's miserable and foggy inland, it's nice here," Cloud said.

They stayed on the beach as long as they could stand the cold wind, picked up some interesting pieces of driftwood and a few shells to take home with them – and agreed to come back again sometime – maybe rent a cabin and spend several days exploring, shopping, and having fun. But for now, they concluded that they would like to get home before it was very late. At this time of year, it got dark quite early so no matter what they'd have to drive in the dark, but at least they'd be home for dinner – maybe.

Later, as they drove off the highway and onto the gravel road that led to André's house, they whole sky seemed to light up. The DC Fire Control trucks were blocking the road. Something is on fire!

22. What the Hell?

Dolly desperately tried to edge her Forester past the sheriff's car and the fire engines, but she finally gave up and parked on the gravel at the side of the road. They all piled out and went running to see what was happening. Miki was instantly frightened for her dogs. Dolly was similarly concerned about Luke's safety.

As they rounded a corner, they could see the fire more clearly and see the firemen trying vainly to put it out. It was the garage. Well, thank heavens it was only the garage! But wait a minute, that's where André had stored all of his paintings and old manuscripts when he moved his bedroom into the studio! André and Luke were standing back by the house so they'd be out of the way of the firefighters. Miki ran up to him and asked him, "Were you able to get anything out of there?"

"No," André said, "it just went up like an inferno. It was a complete holocaust of flames by the time the firefighters got here. It's possible that someone set fire to it on purpose. I don't know what would have been in there that would have exploded into flames that fast."

"Don't you keep your paint and paint thinner and stuff like that in there?"

"Well, yes, but they weren't close to anything that would have been flammable. I had them in a separate cabinet. I just don't know what to think. At least the Escalade wasn't in there. Luke and I were just coming home when we saw the flames."

Sheriff Melville came up to the group and said, "I'm sure sorry about this Mr. Zhalovy. It looks like the fire was so well along that the firefighters never had a chance to save anything in the garage. You're lucky though that they kept the fire from spreading to the house or to the woods."

"Yup, that's for sure," André answered. "Lucky."

"You know anybody who might want to start a fire out here? Or have you seen any strangers around? Maybe those Aryan Nation fellas that like to give people trouble? The fire chief says it looks a lot like arson to him, but he can't be sure until the fire is completely down and cool. By the way, where's that guy who was living here? The Chinese person?"

"Oh, Robert has moved on up to Eugene. I guess he found himself a rich widow up there," André told him.

"What about Henry? Is he around?"

"No. Why would he be? There isn't any work for him around here at this time of year."

"Well," said the sheriff, "Gerry said Henry was talking again about being a member of your family … said that the women told him he was as much a member of the family as they were. And that he could prove it."

"Oh, we were just trying to make him feel good," Miki said. "We didn't really mean anything by it."

"Huh. Well, apparently Henry is wondering why he can't live out here with the rest of the family," the sheriff noted. "Do you know where he lives? Do you think that he'd get mad enough to come out here and set fire to the garage?"

André said, "I have no idea where he lives. I never asked him. He just came wandering by almost every day and did whatever chores I had for him. He did a good job. I can't complain, and I don't think I ever saw him angry with anyone. Can any of you?"

No, huh-uh, and shaking of heads were the general answers of the whole group. "He was always willing and ready to do anything he was asked to do as far as I know," Cloud said, "He wouldn't have any reason to do this – set a fire, I mean."

"Well, like I said, we have to wait until the fire is completely out and cold before we can get in there to investigate," Sheriff Melville said, "I may have some more questions for all of you when that time comes. And I'll try to have a little chat with those Aryan Nation people – though they tend to disappear into thin air whenever I want to see them."

They all watched until the firemen were finished and marveled at the wreck that was left of the garage. It looked like a war zone. No one could go in, of course, until after the fire inspectors and the sheriff were finished with their investigation, but it was clear that all of André's precious things were gone in the fire.

Miki and Cloud just automatically held hands with André as they walked back to the house. He looked down at their hands and thanked them. Luke built a nice, warm fire in the fireplace while the women got busy in the kitchen and put together a quick but hot meal of vegetable soup and fresh corn bread plus hot coffee and tea. The family sat around the fire eating from their laps or from the coffee table or whatever was handy.

They were a gloomy bunch of people, but strangely they finally felt like a family. They all looked at André as the alpha male – not necessarily as father. All the women were sisters – as different as can be, but sisters – and Luke was their son & nephew.

Finally, to break the mood a bit, Dolly asked, "Well, how shall we celebrate Luke's birthday – since he has decided he will not have a Bar Mitzvah."

"Oh he has? I didn't know," André said, "You might re-think that Luke. It would have been very important to Dorothy and her husband, I'm sure."

"Yeah, I know," Luke said, "But I didn't really know them much, and I can't remember my dad at all. I don't feel like a Jew. I feel like Mom's kid – whatever that is."

"Well, how would you like to celebrate then?" Dolly inquired.

"Let's go to the Chinese Buffet where I can eat as much as I want," Luke suggested.

"They'll go out of business if they feed you was much as you want!" Dolly laughed.

"I miss being able to go to that place back home that had the 'Killer Chocolate Cake.' And to Coldstone Creamery for ice cream."

"Yeah, and to the coffee house – Sufficient Grounds it was called. Oh well." Dolly said and then asked, "What do the rest of you miss about being at home?"

Cloud said, "I don't miss a thing – no stepfather trying to touch me every time my mother wasn't at home. No mother saying that I made the whole thing up. That's why I came up here to live with Aunt Gerry, but I don't miss her either. I mean, she's great, you know, but I'd rather be with you guys."

Joy said, "You know what I miss? I miss the fine restaurants in San Francisco and the dressing up to go out. You know, putting on the dog, as they say – four inch heels, sheer stockings, fancy dresses, and lots of jewelry. I miss that, and I miss shopping at Nordstrom's and at Neiman Marcus. But I only really miss them occasionally. Most of the time, I feel so relaxed here – no stress, no deadlines, no meetings, no endless phone calls! That is very pleasant. And I even enjoy wearing loose, comfortable clothes – like these sweatshirts."

Dolly said, "Oh that reminds me of something! I'll be right back." And she dashed outside to her car. When she came back, she was carrying the package with the two sweatshirts – one a size Large for a growing Luke and the other an Extra Large for André.

Luke liked his very much – black with *"I've been to BANDON"* on the front. André looked at his, which was exactly the same, and turned his head as he wiped away a stray tear or two. "Thank you. This is great," he said.

Miki broke the serious mood again by saying, "I don't miss a thing about Los Angeles, and if I ever tell anyone that I'm going back there, please take me to a shrink or lock me up right away!"

Everyone laughed and asked "Why?"

Miki said, "It's hot, dirty, and crime-ridden. I guess if you're rich it might be nice. You'd have a huge air-conditioned house with a huge swimming pool. And you'd go from there in your air-conditioned car to your air-conditioned office, or club, or whatever. But for mere mortals like most of us, it's just hot, and it's dangerous! I drove everyday from the Valley – the San Fernando Valley – through L.A. to East L.A. to teach mathematics to a bunch of heathens. That's nuts! None of them wanted to learn it, and if my old Volvo had broken down on the way, I'd have had to sit locked in my car until some trustworthy looking person came along to help me.

"Of course," she added, "Nowadays, with cell phones I could at least have called one of my roommates or Triple A or 911, but for most of my career, I would have been trapped like a juicy, fat white morsel in that car with no one but gangs and skinheads around."

"Wow! You make it sound awful. Surely it couldn't have been that bad," Dolly said.

"Oh, yes, it really was. My time in L.A. now feels like it was a jail sentence. If I hadn't had my cute little house, my dogs, and my great roommates to go home to at night, I might have left much sooner than I did. But I had tenure, you see. I was top of the totem pole so to speak. So I stuck it out. But I sure am glad to be here now. I feel like a brand new person here. And I feel like a part of a family here, don't you?" Miki asked everyone in general.

"Yes, I guess that's what we are – a very strange family – we're all so different in so many ways," Joy said.

Luke offered, "I don't think we're all that different. Sure we're all different religions and stuff like that, but, gee, we don't go to church anyway – so what difference does it make? Joy looks a little different because she's half Chinese, but Miki looks a little different because she's half Irish. And Cloud, you gotta admit that you look a little different!"

Cloud laughed along with everyone else and agreed that they were all a little different but alike, too. It was good to be able to laugh a little in spite of what had just happened to them.

23. The Investigation

Yellow crime scene tape went up around the garage and the area just next to it. Soon the fire investigators were back and covered every inch of the fire territory and all around the outside of it. A fire investigator looked at the fire remains, and obtained information to reconstruct the sequence of events leading up to the fire. They took their time and were very thorough.

A few days later, Sheriff Melville stopped by to tell André, "We have finished the investigation. And we really cannot tell for sure whether the fire was a case of arson or not. It surely looks like arson, but there were so many volatile things stored out there. We are pretty sure where the fire started, but we cannot swear in a court of law *how* it started."

"Where did it start, Sheriff?" André wanted to know.

"Looks like it started right next to a stack of paintings on the west wall. Does that mean anything in particular to you?"

André though about it and said, "Oh, I don't know. Those were the nudes – my favorites. Maybe if somebody really hated me, they'd start with my favorites, but I don't know who would know that."

"Well, I wish I could give you a better answer, but at least now you can get a crime report and put in an insurance claim, clear away the mess and build a new garage. However, just between you and me, I'm gonna continue the investigation awhile. I want to talk to Henry and maybe to some of the Cunningham's kinfolk, including Pastor Grosshaus."

"Thank you, Sheriff, I appreciate what you are doing," André said.

The sheriff went back to town and asked Gerry, "Hey, could you please be on the lookout for Henry and send him over to see me next time you see him? I just wanna ask him a couple of questions – nothin' serious."

"Sure," Gerry said, "You still investigating the big fire out at André's?"

"Sort of. Why?"

"Well, you ought to talk to the Kincaid boys. They're kin to the Cunningham brothers, and I heard they were mighty mad when Don and Gary got sent up."

"Thanks, Gerry, I'll do that. By the way, have you seen Pastor Grosshaus around town lately?" the sheriff asked.

"Sure. He drives that big mean black Hummer down main street everyday – probably looking for someone smiling or doing something else sinful like that!"

"Is he that bad?"

"Sure is. He's suspicious of anybody who's happy. Says they must be doing somethin' wrong!"

"Well, maybe I'll have a talk with him, too."

That very afternoon, the sheriff had occasion to run into Pastor Grosshaus as he drove into town and parked his H2 in back of the big old steel building where his group was said to have its meetings. No one would say what the meetings were about or even who attended the meetings, but it was widely believed that they were a neo-Nazi or Aryan Nation group. All of

them wore black from head to foot and the "pastor" was a huge man of about three hundred-fifty pounds with a permanently sour look on his face. He was also rude to just about everyone – and did not keep it a secret how he felt about Jews, African-Americans, homosexuals, Mexicans, and Arabs. In fact, if you did not have a light complexion and blue or green eyes, you were mighty suspect as far as Pastor Grosshaus was concerned.

The sheriff walked over to him and greeted him, "Hello there, Dick, how're you doin'?"

"Sheriff. I'm doin' just fine. Thank you for askin'. But I've never known you to be curious about my health. Whatcha want?"

"Well, Dick, I'm lookin' into an arson fire out to Mr. Zhalovy's place. You wouldn't know anything about that, would you?"

"A fire?" the Pastor said, "I hadn't heard about a fire. Hmmm. Anybody hurt? Any loss?"

"Well, the garage was a totally loss, but fortunately, no one was hurt and the house and the woods were okay, too. Yup. It was a shame. Do you have any idea who might want to do such a thing, Dick?"

"You know, I have no idea. And I also have no idea why you're asking me about it," the pastor said. "Oh, and, by the way, I don't like you callin' me Dick.

People call me Pastor Grosshaus or Brother Grosshaus."

"Yes, I imagine they do. Sorry, Dick."

"And when is it that you come up for election again, John?"

"Don't fret, Dick, I'm not running this time. I'm getting' too old for this crazy business."

The two men parted. The sheriff walked back to his patrol car, and Pastor Grosshaus watched him all the way with a frown and a sneer.

Henry came by the sheriff's office later the same day. He said, "Gerry told me to come here. Have I done somethin' wrong, Mr. Melville?"

"No, I don't think so, Henry, but I have to talk to everyone who might know anything about that fire out at Mr. Zhalovy's garage. You know anything about that, Henry?"

"Gollee! No. I heard about the fire though. I heard that someone set it on purpose. Is that right?"

"It looks that way, Henry. And I also know that you were pretty mad at Mr. Zhalovy because he wouldn't let you come out and live at his place with his family. I heard that you said you were as much as part of his family as anyone else."

"That's true, Mr. Melville. I did say that, and I kin prove it! But I'd never do anything to hurt Mr. Zhalovy or anyone out there. Honest, I wouldn't."

"Did you know that Mr. Zhalovy had stored all of his paintings and manuscripts out in the garage? Did you know that a lot of the paintings were of nude women?"

"Yeah, I knew that, but I never looked at them. I ain't never seen a neked woman. My mama said it would turn me blind – or somethin'," Henry muttered and looked down at his feet.

"Okay, Henry, I believe you. I really do." The sheriff paused and then asked, "Where do you live anyway, Henry? Nobody around seems to know where you live."

"I have me a cabin that I built. It's real nice – 'cept it doesn't have a bathroom. I take a bath in the river once in a while, and I have a privy though. But it's cold in the winter, and I'm getting' older, you know. That's why I wanted to move in with Mr. Zhalovy and the rest of our family."

"Well, now Henry, don't you go botherin' those folks. Okay? If it gets too cold where you live, you can always come in to the mission, you know. They have nice warm beds and make a good hot supper every night for folks like you," the sheriff advised.

"Yup. Okay," Henry muttered as he shuffled off for his daily pie and ice cream at Gerry's Diner. He reckoned he'd have peach pie this night – yeah, hot peach pie with vanilla ice cream and a cup of coffee.

At the same time, the sheriff straightened up the papers on his desk, turned off his computer, and decided to call it a day. He told his deputy to keep an eye on things because it was possible that he'd made an enemy of Pastor Grosshaus today – on purpose.

He dropped by the Kincaid place on the way home. They were just sitting down to dinner and were a little vexed to be bothered for no apparent reason. Sheriff Melville asked briefly about the night of the fire and got alibis from everyone. He would check those later, but the Kincaids didn't seem to have any particular grudge against André. They thought the cousins Cunningham "had it comin'."

24. History & Hammers

Cloud finally had her cast removed and said she felt at least ten pounds lighter – but that her leg looked "fish-belly white" and ugly. Joy encouraged her to shave it and rub on some of the leg makeup that she had brought with her and always used in the winter. She told Cloud that she would look like she had a suntan in November! Cloud rubbed the makeup on the leg that had shrunken a little, and it immediately turned a horrible orange color. So she decided that she could put it on both legs, and they'd both be orange … or she could just wash it off and look almost normal.

The entire group celebrated Luke's thirteenth birthday at the Chinese Buffet as he had requested. Everyone got a lot of pleasure out of watching Luke fill and refill his plate with about three times as much as most of them ate. He especially liked the noodles, the coconut shrimp, the beef broccoli, and the hot and spicy General Tso's chicken.

André said, "Well, he got our money's worth, didn't he?"

Dolly answered, "It's always a good idea to take a teenager to a buffet or any kind of all-you-can-eat place."

When they got home, they found that Cloud had baked a big chocolate cake and had cookie dough ice cream to go with it. And in spite of being already stuffed with Chinese food, they each had a little piece of cake and ice cream after Luke made his wish and blew out the thirteen candles on the cake.

"Thank you all for making this a very special birthday. And, yes, Mom, I will write to Grandma and Grandpa and thank them for the books. I will also tell them what I have learned so far. While I'm at it, thank you all for the other presents. Do I have to write to each one of you, too?" Luke asked and then went on, "I am really, really glad to have the new eye pieces and filters for my telescope and the new case to keep them in. They are way wicked!"

After that, life went along as usual. Miki offered to help Luke with algebra, and once in awhile they would sit down together to discuss a particularly obscure problem. Joy offered to help him with English since she had been an English major, but he didn't seem to need any help with that at least not at the moment. Dolly even offered to help with biology – at least the botany part when they got to that – so he had all the tutors and helpers he could possibly use, and he did allow them to drill him on his Spanish vocabulary.

handsome	guapo

Dolly made flash cards – new ones each time he had a new vocabulary list with the English word on one side and the Spanish on the other. The women would take turns drilling him – though none of them knew what the Spanish pronunciation should be (except Luke, of course). André said he could help with Luke's world history studies, and Luke laughingly told his mother that André was probably old enough to <u>remember</u> most of it!

But in actuality, André was a big help to him especially when it came to discussing Attila the Hun,

Alexander the Great, Genghis Khan, Julius Caesar, Galileo, and other ancient heroes and villains. André had made quite a study of many of these people for his own writings, and was able to make them come alive for Luke. Thus, history was no longer just a boring series of dates and battles. It was people – real people who lived, loved, and died. History had color when André talked about it. Why didn't his teacher tell the stories this way? He wondered about that because kids would learn history so much better this way. It was like adding the "color" guy when announcing the football game instead of just talking about scores and statistics.

The family was coming together. It was a nice, mostly peaceful life. André didn't worry about the fire. He knew that Sheriff Melville would stay on top of that and find out what happened if anybody could. But he did think about hiring a security service or getting a bigger, meaner dog that could stay out at night and wouldn't be in danger from cougars or bears or even Dick Grosshaus and his kind.

He'd looked up guard dogs online and was torn between a Komondor, a Kuvasz, or a Rhodesian Ridgeback. However, he knew he just didn't have the skill or the time to train such a dog, and it wasn't going to be possible to fence the entire area. Maybe he'd just fence the living area – around the house, the guest houses, and the new garage. Well, in any case it was time to get on with rebuilding the garage. It's not good to leave the vehicles out in the rain and snow all winter.

André thought about it a long time but finally contacted Gerry and asked her to send Henry on out. He turned up the next day asking for Mr. André, and André asked him, "I need a new garage built, Henry. Can you handle a job that size, or should I get that contractor back out here … the one who did the bathroom and the stairs?"

Henry smiled his lopsided smile and said, "Sure I kin do a garage, Mr. André. You want it the same as the other one – the one that got burnt?"

"Yes, I need a three car garage so that we have room for the vehicles as well as some storage. Or maybe even a four car garage. Can you make a drawing and a list of supplies and show it to me, Henry?"

"A drawing, huh? I don't reckon I've ever made a drawing. I just measure things out and build. I never needed a drawing afore," Henry said quietly, scratching his head.

"Well, I'd like to see a drawing. You can come into my study, and we'll work on it together if you want to. Would that be okay, Henry?"

"Oh, you betcha. I'd like to come into your study, Mr. André – and work with you on a drawing – you betcha!"

So the two men went into the house and up the

new spiral staircase to the second floor. Henry marveled at the staircase and said it looked like a stretched out slinky toy. In the study, André laid out a piece graph paper on a big drawing table which had been folded against the wall in order to make room for his bed and other bedroom furniture. He got out a big three-sided ruler that he called a scale, a straight edge, some triangular plastic things, and some fancy mechanical pencils.

"Okay," he said, "let's start by deciding on our scale. Say we do one inch equals one foot. That would mean that we would need a piece of paper forty inches wide in order to draw a forty foot garage, wouldn't we?"

"Yessir, Mr. André, I 'spect so."

"But we don't have paper that wide. Our paper is seventeen inches by twenty-two inches. And the normal scale that most folks use is one quarter inch to the foot. So if I draw a line one inch long, that would be equal to four feet on the actual building. Do you understand that, Henry?"

"Uh, I think so … mebbe," Henry said.

"Okay now watch. I'll draw a line to represent one of the long walls of the garage. I'll draw the line ten inches long to represent the forty-foot side of the building," André instructed, and then using a straight edge, he drew a line on the paper. "Now, Henry, we want the next side of the building to be twenty feet. So how long should I draw this line?"

Henry looked at the back of André's head as he leaned over the drawing and suddenly had a mental picture of a hammer and using it as hard as he could on the back of the head in front of him. He shook himself a bit and said, "I dunno, Mr. André. How long?"

"Well, come on, Henry, if ten inches represents forty feet, wouldn't five inches represent twenty feet? That makes sense, doesn't it? And then the side opposite would also be five inches, and the last line that would connect the whole thing up would be ten inches. Now, we have a rectangle twice as long as it is wide. So the big hanging doors should go on the long side and windows on the short sides or maybe a door and more windows on the back. So we also need to draw those features so we can figure out the length and quantity of lumber to be used."

Again Henry saw visions of a hammer and a smashed head with lots of blood swimming in his vision. He shook his head and closed his eyes.

"Henry, I do think we may have to hire a contractor to do the garage. I think it may be a bit much for you. Do you agree?" André said.

"I dunno. I wanna do it, but I don't understand this drawing thing. I don't see how ten inches can be the side of a garage. I don't see why we don't just lay out the plan on the ground and build up from there," Henry said.

"Well, because it wouldn't be right. It wouldn't be good enough. It has to have careful planning just like anything else that you want to come out right."

"Do ya just throw out anything that ain't right?" Henry asked.

"Well, sometimes. Yes, I guess I do because I like things to be right. Are you feeling okay, Henry. You look a little flushed – a little red in the face."

"Sure. Yeah. I'm okay. I wanna ask you something.' Mr. André," Henry said standing right up to the other man.

"Fine. Henry. You ask anything you want."

"Why do you have all these women living here with you? I don't mean Cloud. I know about Cloud. I mean the others – and that boy, too."

"Why, they're my family, Henry. It took me a long time to find them. I didn't know anything about them, but I hired a detective and he found all my children – all living in California in different places, and now they live here with me so we can be a family," André explained.

"So how do you know that you don't have more family somewhere?"

"I guess I don't, Henry. But the group that is here now makes for a nice family, and I'm contented. Why do you ask? Is it because those girls told you that you were part of the family? You don't believe that, do you, Henry?"

"I dunno. I guess not. I'm not like them, am I? I'm slow. Oh, I know it. Even Mama said I was dumb and foolish. But ken I come out here and live with you guys and be part of the family anyhow?" Henry asked, "I mean even though I'm not like the rest of them?"

"Henry, I don't have room to let just anybody live out here. Don't you think it's enough that there are six of us out here now?"

"One more would only make seven. See I do know my numbers," Henry said, "and I can read but just not very fast. I'm as good as anybody. That's what I think. And my Mama told me – well, she told me that the man on the back of the books was my Daddy. That's you Mr. André. She said you were my Daddy, and I believed her."

"Oh my God, Henry. You can't be sure she meant me. There are lots of men on lots of books."

"You wait, I'll bring you a picture. Then you'll see," Henry said and then left.

André later told everyone at dinner about his conversation with Henry. He admitted that Henry did seem a little unhinged and wondered whether he ought to tell Sheriff Melville.

Miki thought, "He's just sort of slow and naive – maybe even childlike. I don't think he's at all threatening."

Joy agreed, "Yes, Henry is sort of innocent and maybe retarded, but I think he's harmless."

Since they all came to a sort of agreement that Henry was innocuous, André decided to keep Sheriff Melville out of their personal lives. So they moved on with daily life and decided it was time to think about Thanksgiving and make plans for that.

Cloud wanted to do the whole turkey dinner and pumpkin pie thing. Joy said they should have some fresh shrimp and sea scallops and maybe duck. Luke said that was just not American. He explained, "Americans eat turkey, stuffing, mashed potatoes, gravy and pumpkin pie – and then they watch football. That's how it's done."

Dolly said, "I didn't hear any mention of vegetables in there, young man. You have to have vegetables whether you like it or not – maybe a green bean casserole. You know, the kind that has the mushroom soup and canned onions on top."

"I guess that would be okay," Luke said, "Oh! Oh, and cranberry sauce. I like the kind that comes in a can. I like to push in out so it still has the shape of the can."

"Fine," Miki said. "It all sounds wonderful to me. Be sure to get a big fat turkey. I like the dark meat best, but I like the breast meat for sandwiches the next day. Shall I invite Dr. Wayne to join us? Whatcha think?"

"Of course, that would be very nice. And I wonder, should we invite Henry to the dinner?" André asked.

"Oh, I don't know. Doesn't it seem like he's trouble enough already?" Joy said.

"Yeah," Luke said, "but I think he lives all alone. I don't think he has any family here. He'd just end up going to Gerry's for pie probably."

"Well, let me think about it," André said. "He'll be back around soon, I'm sure."

25. Denouement

Expect perfection and revile the missed mark.

Henry did come back. He came back to show André two pieces of worn paper that he'd had hidden in his most prized possession box – along with marbles, buttons, foreign coins, and other oddities that he'd found over the years. But these two papers were the most important things in his life.

He knocked on the front door of the house as the family was setting up the table for their Thanksgiving dinner. Cloud opened the door, and said, "Hello Henry, you here for Thanksgiving dinner? It's still about an hour away, but come on in and have a glass of hot spiced cider with us."

Henry murmured, "Thank you, Miss Cloud, but I'm here to see Mr. André, if he's here."

"That's fine, Henry. He's here. Come on in."

As Henry entered the house, André stood up and greeted him. "Hello Henry. I don't guess we were exactly expecting you, but I'm sure that the women here have made enough dinner for a whole army. So you'll stay for dinner, won't you?"

Again Henry mumbled, "I have somethin' to show you, Mr. André."

"Okay, Henry, let's see it."

"No. Not here – upstairs in your office or whatever it is," Henry insisted.

"Fine," André agreed and led the way up the staircase and into his studio/bedroom.

ANDRÉ ZHALOVY was born in Russia in 1933. He once worked for the KGB in Israel and spent some time in a Chinese prison. He has written 17 spy thrillers, many of which include his personal experiences. André and his wife, Vivienne, currently live in the Pacific Northwest.

Henry smoothed out the first piece of paper and laid it in front of André on the drawing table. It was a picture from the back of one of André's last books, and it showed an old unsmiling André … an unhappy André no longer sure of his talent and no longer feeling his manhood.

Henry told him, "My Mama showed me this and told me that this was my daddy. She said you looked a lot different when you were young, and she had no idea where you lived or what you were doing now. She just knew that you went off to the war and left her at home – knocked up."

"What? I mean, who is your mother, Henry? Where does she live?"

"She don't live at all anymore. She's dead. But her name was Betsy Clark, and she used to live in

Concord in California. She went to high school there, she said. Do you remember her now?"

"Betsy? Betsy. Hmmm. Of course, high school Betsy! How could I forget? It was such an awfully long time ago. How old are you, Henry?" André inquired.

"I'm fifty-seven – gonna be fifty-eight in February."

"Jesus Christ! You really could be my kid. I had no idea. I didn't know Betsy was pregnant when I left, and I never saw her again after I came back. How'd you find me anyway, Henry?"

That's when Henry laid out the other piece of paper and smoothed it on top of the table. It was a newspaper article from the San Francisco Chronicle, dated June 16, 1999. It was a wedding announcement for Vivienne Audier-Ridgeway and Mr. André Zhalovy with a nice picture of the happy bride.

Audier-Ridgeway and Zhalovy Nuptials Celebrated

Dressed in an ivory designer brocade suit, popular San Francisco socialite, Vivienne Audier-Ridgeway today because the bride of André Zhalovy, the world-famous writer and artist. The wedding was performed by Mayor Willie Brown. Witnesses were Vivienne's daughter and her husband, Mr. & Mrs. Marc Gibson. The happy couple plan to honeymoon in the South Pacific islands and then retire to Vivienne's estate in Oregon.

"And that's how I found you, Mr. André. I followed the Audier-Ridgeway woman you married until I found where her "estate' was at. I built myself a cabin up in the hills not far from here. I built it out of wood your builders just threw away because it weren't perfect. And I decided to just leave you alone and see what would happen.

"I was sorry when Mrs. Vivienne died. She was a real lady. And I was glad when you got Cloud to come out and work for you. You needed that. But it kinda got me mad when I saw all these other people movin' in with you. 'Specially when Gerry said they were your family, as if I'm not! And me still out there in that cold old cabin.

"I guess you don't think I'm good enough to be your kin. I guess you think I'm not perfect. I'm like the other stuff you just throw away." Henry finally finished and took a long breath.

André looked long and hard at the picture and the newspaper article. He looked long and hard at Henry, and said, "Well, this doesn't really prove anything, Henry. Your mother could have made up any sort of story just so you'd think you had a daddy somewhere that she could identify out of all the men she might have been with."

"You callin' my mama a bad girl – a whore or somethin'? You got no call to do that," Henry said, and he pulled out the hammer he had inside his overalls. But as Henry raised the hammer to smash it into André's brain, he had a sudden vision of gushing, pooling blood. He gagged. He doubled over. He dropped the hammer. He vomited. He vomited all over André and all over the floor.

The strange strangled sounds brought Dolly and Luke running up the stairs to see what was going on.

André was just thumping Henry on the back, and asking him if he was okay.

Dolly said, "What the Hell? What happened?"

André calmly said, "Henry was just feeling a little sickly. He was showing me some ideas he had and demonstrating them with his hammer here. Don't worry. He and I will clean up the mess, and we'll be down in a little while."

With that Dolly and Luke backed out of the room while André got a wet washcloth from the bathroom and wiped Henry's face and hands. Cloud brought up a roll of paper towels and just glanced at the filth and the men as the two stooped together to clean up a mess on the table and on André. When the floor was clean enough to suit them, the two men went into the bathroom together to wash up.

Henry said, "Ya know, I was gonna kill you with that hammer. I told myself that unless you confessed that you was my daddy, I'd kill ya."

"I know that, Henry. At least I know it now. And I'm proud of you that you couldn't bring yourself to do it. If I'm your daddy – which I very well might be – then you'd be within your rights to kill me for ignoring you for fifty-seven … almost fifty-eight years."

"But killin' ain't never right, is it, Mr. André?"

"No. Well, not usually. Sometimes we have to kill when we are being attacked or to shelter our loved ones or to have food or something like that. But just killing because you're angry or excited sure isn't right."

André put on clean clothes and found a robe and slippers that Henry could wear temporarily until he could get his shirt and overalls washed and his shoes cleaned up. (Henry was much bigger than André and couldn't fit into any of his clothes.) André took everything downstairs as the whole group stared at the two men. André threw out the trash and put all the dirty clothes together into the washing machine.

Then he offered Henry a cup of hot, spiced cider and announced to all that Henry would be staying for dinner. "He was a little sickly a while ago, but he's okay now," André said.

"That's great," Luke said, "I'll help Cloud set another place at the table." He strode off towards the kitchen and announced, "We shall be eight – for dinner."

They had a wonderful dinner: roast turkey, bread stuffing with sausage and nuts, mashed potatoes, giblet gravy, cranberry sauce (the kind that Luke could push out of the can), green bean casserole, green and black olives, pickles, homemade dinner rolls with real butter, a nice white wine, pumpkin pie with whipped cream and coffee. It was a very American Thanksgiving … just the way Luke had envisioned it.

And the conversation was lively as well. André started the chat by saying, "I think Henry is going to move here with us. I'd like to put him up in the room next to mine. That is, if you don't mind moving out to what used to be Robert's cottage, Cloud."

"Mind? Heck no, I don't mind. I've been wanting to move out there, Cloud said.

"Are we sure that Robert isn't coming back?" Joy inquired.

André said (between mouthfuls), "I think we're about as sure as we're likely to get. But, you know, I was also thinking of building an apartment over the new garage. It would be a good place for me maybe – or for Robert if he does come back. However, the last I heard from him, he was thinking of marrying the Eugene cutie."

"Well, good for him," Miki said and blushed lightly as she glanced at Dr. Wayne.

"Yeah, well I hope he's happy this time. He's too old to be going from woman to woman anymore." André said.

"Oh, yeah? You too old, too, Grandpa?" Luke asked.

"Grandpa? Grandpa! I sort of like the sound of that, young man. Yup, that's good."

"No, it's 'wicked,' Grandpa!"

"Just look at this family, André," Miki said, "You couldn't get a more diverse group – more contrast than this – well, maybe you could, but this is contrast enough. Let's see … there's me, Miki, a pink-faced, pudgy, middle-aged Catholic and my friend, the admirable Dr. Roger Wayne. Then there's thin and elegant Chinese-American, Joy. Plus a much younger hard-working forester, Dolly, and her 'wicked' son, Luke Skywalker Lerner. A barely old enough to drink and somewhat mysterious Cloud, and a guileless but colorful older brother, Henry."

"Don't forget the older-than-dirt father of most all of this bunch." André added.

Joy broke in, "If you're middle aged, Miki, what does that make me?"

"Mature," Miki said and they all laughed politely.

"So how do you feel about being part of this group, Henry?" Luke asked.

"Good … mighty good. I ain't never had no family, and now I do. It's like the happy ending of a movie on TV … like Bonanza or somethin'."

(Did they live happily ever after? Are you kidding?)

Bibliography:

[i] From www.arts-fine.co.uk by D.R. Durkin

[ii] Bach, Richard, Illusions – the Adventures of a Reluctant Messiah, "Reminders for the Advanced Soul, Dell Publishing, 1977.

[iii] Leslie Gore.

[iv] Fforde, Jasper: The Eyre Affair and Lost in a Good Book and others.

[v] Local Area Network.

[vi] Tim Kosderka, Forest Manager, Roseburg District, Weyerhaeuser Company. 07/24/09.

[vii] http://www.ehow.com/how_2132114_remove-porcupine-quills-dog.html, 07/16/09.

[viii] www.catholic.org/prayers, 07/20/09.

[ix] Leopold, Aldo, The Sand County Almanac, Oxford University Press, New York. 1966, pg. 68.

[x] Helen Hunt Jackson (1830-1885), U.S. writer ("H. H."; "Saxe Holm"). October's Bright Blue Weather (l. 1-4). . . Family Book of Best Loved Poems, The. David L. George, ed. (1952) Doubleday & Company.

[xi] www.goodreads.com/quotes, 07/23/09.

Watch for the sequel coming soon: <u>The Box in the Attic</u>

4744555R0

Made in the USA
Charleston, SC
10 March 2010